SIXTEEN OF THE BEST

A collection of sixteen prize-winning adult discipline short stories selected by Sarah Veitch over four years of Palmprint's international writing competition

First published in 2007 by
Palmprint Publications
PO Box 392
Weston-super-Mare
BS23 3ZS
United Kingdom
www.palmprint.co.uk

Collection copyright © 2007 by Sarah Veitch.
Copyright of individual stories rests with each author.

The rights of the authors of this work have been asserted in accordance with the Copyright, Designs and Patents Act 1988.

All characters in this book are fictitious and any resemblance to real persons, living or dead, is purely coincidental.

All rights reserved. No part of this publication may be reproduced, transmitted or stored in a retrieval system, in any form or by any means without the express permission in writing of Palmprint Publications having first been obtained.

This book is sold on the condition that it shall not, by way of trade or otherwise, be lent, resold, hired out or otherwise circulated without the publisher's prior written consent in any form of binding or cover other than that in which it is published and without a similar condition being imposed on the subsequent purchaser.

ISBN-10: 0-9537953-5-7
ISBN-13: 978-0-9537953-5-2

Printed and bound in Great Britain.

Characters in books act without risk – but in the real world please practice safe sex.

SIXTEEN OF THE BEST

Edited by Sarah Veitch

Contents

L'Ancien Régime — 1
  Michael Redbrick

Goddess — 13
  Tulsa Brown

Way Out West — 27
  Suzee Moon and Stan Strap

A New Understanding — 41
  Pearl Jones

Cat Fight at the Lucky Seven — 55
  Stan Strap

Disobedience à la carte — 67
  Kit

Disobedience, Passion and the Unjust Whip — 75
  J.D. Jensen

Broken Vows — 91
  Ruby Kola

The Mercy of Strange Men — 103
  Aimee Nichols

Lessons — 117
  Alicia Wag

Beloved Birch James Baron	129
The Key to the Unknown Sarah Dean	143
Think Pink Bruce Anderson	157
Rubious – The Colour of Rubies Mark Ramsden	173
Come Here Katharine Tyler Brooks	181
How Not to Manage Debt Jean Roberta	189
Hard Times Sarah Veitch	203
For Writers Only	219
About the Authors	231

Introduction

A bare bottom served up for punishment will always give the discerning reader an erotic charge, and there's no shortage of such reluctantly-exposed flesh in this collection. There's also a diverse range of settings and themes. These stories resulted from Palmprint's international cash prize spanking fiction competitions, the stories chosen solely on merit over four discerning years, with winning authors coming from Australia, Canada, England, Scotland, USA and Wales.

We're in the firm hands of the overseer at a women's reformatory in the highly arousing *L'Ancien Régime*. He gloats over each miscreant's punishment: 'She knows she cannot win and her agonised buttocks will turn her into a dancing puppet, wheedling and beseeching to be spared.'

It's the man who begs to be spared in *Goddess*, the only woman-on-top piece in this mainly female submissive collection. Dan submits to the ritual of punishment until 'All the tortured waiting, teasing, misery and urgent hunger spun together in a white sphere' in this hypnotic detective tale.

The next story, *Way Out West*, utilises humour in addition to the nerve-tingling caning scenes. Suzee angers the local sheriff, Stan, who has no choice but to raise her skirts and smartly apply his palm, incrementally increasing her humiliation. 'I don't think she is learning her lesson. I think we'll have those drawers undone. See how she likes it on the bare.'

Back to the present day with *A New Understanding* about the psychological and physiological aspects of CP. 'A more serious caress followed, and I think I briefly lost my mind, too desperate to come to consider, to care, to breathe. He obliged my need, slicking fingers on either side of my clit, pinching and twisting and stroking, his other hand thrusting inward and up, hard, until I came.'

Hands are again applied to rumps in *Cat Fight at the Lucky Seven*, but it's not enough to turn the local women into good girls. So Stan, who we met earlier in *Way Out West*, has to apply a willow switch: 'Stan surveyed his work with some satisfaction. Suzee's bottom was bright red with a series of dark lines across her trembling cheeks.'

It's breasts which are reddened in *Disobedience à la carte*, a perfectly-realised study of a CP relationship. 'The anticipation of the whip, the pain, the punishment is almost unbearable. My nipples press against the rain-wet tee-shirt, my pelvis moves in spasms against the cunt-wet knickers.'

Whips also figure in *Disobedience, Passion and the Unjust Whip* when slave girl Aquistana is sent to an inquisitor to be taught a painful lesson. 'Such crude disrobing had been shocking to her, and the humiliation made her face burn hotly. But she knew there was nothing she could do to entirely conceal her intimate places.'

We're transported to a strict academy in *Broken Vows* where the unfortunate Miss Williams is soundly tawsed by her collegiate colleagues. Fortunately there are consolations: 'She was aroused but sore at the same time, wanting him to enter her, to finger her into a deep long orgasm.'

There's also sexual arousal, as well as profound humiliation, in *The Mercy of Strange Men* when Lydia is displayed, naked, to a roomful of appreciative onlookers and has her bottom beaten with a riding crop. It's the epitome of pain-pleasure: 'He begins to spank her in time with his thrusts, and she writhes below him, not knowing whether to beg him to stop or insist that he never does.'

Never say never is also the mantra of the student submissive in *Lessons* as her dominant lecturer takes her mind and body to the limit: 'She could feel every inch of his fingers leaving their mark, branding her. The skin of her ass stung and tingled.'

The main character in *Beloved Birch* also ends up with a sore arse, but in this case he's an eighteen year old vandal who has been sentenced to a judicial birching. As he is submissive, this is his wildest wet dream, 'A swish in the air and the birch struck the centre of his buttocks with a slashing whip-like crack. An exquisite lance of pain seared across his behind and he shuddered with pleasure.'

There's an equally exquisite test for Beth in *The Key to the Unknown* when her lover fits her with a chastity belt and arranges for her to be corrected by a range of increasingly-demanding men and women: 'Often he lashed me to the central pillar in the music room and used his favourite – a vicious cat-o'-nine-tails. The leather thongs licked up between the crack in my buttocks and stung my tenderest skin.'

There's further well-warmed skin in *Think Pink* when youthful presenter Suzie Starr enrages her environmentally-friendly producer and earns herself a thorough tanning. 'Hoisting her more firmly across his lap, he began to lash her naked contours. He slapped for all the times she'd taken part in some stupid show with an alliterative title. He slapped to punish her for contributing to dumbed-down TV. He watched dispassionately as she jerked and kicked and implored him, as she desperately tried to rise up and push his fingers away.'

Colour also features prominently in *Rubious – The Colour of Rubies* where a pretty Gothic brunette meets a submissive Russian woman. 'I usually ask a receiver to kiss the paddle before and after use. Sometimes I douse the surface with water because it makes an already tender bottom much more sensitive to the smacking leather impact. And because moist reddening cheeks look even more enticing.'

A hand and a strap are employed in *Come Here* when a man disciplines his female lover for lying to him. 'Naked now except for her high heels and stockings, she waited for his next move, trembling both from the spanking she had just received and what more was to come.'

Emily has it coming after she takes money from the Kinky Teachers Club in *How Not to Manage Debt*. The disciplinary committee take her to task and make her strip: 'Calloused, knowing hands ran down my sides and familiarly over my buttocks, making me squirm. I jerked when a hard male belly and a harder cock pressed into my back as a different pair of hands squeezed my breasts.'

Bringing up the rear, so to speak, is my own story, *Hard Times*, set in a nineteenth century women's prison. Constance enrages the warden with her airs and graces and is sent to the punishment hall and fettered to the birching frame. 'He picked up the punisher again, knowing that this was his favourite part of the session, the second half. By now, the girl bent over the frame knew exactly what a thrashing felt like, was desperate for respite. He only had to scrape the birch against the ground – as he was doing with the paddle now – for the troublemaker to pucker up her disarmed bare bottom. He only had to move his arm and make the air currents change for her to push herself desperately against the metal bar.'

So there we have it – sixteen of the best plus my own humble contribution. I hope that you enjoy reading these prize-winning stories as much as I enjoyed editing them.

Sarah Veitch

L'Ancien Régime

Michaël Redbrick

On the tenth anniversary of his appointment, the Proctor of Women's Quarters at Westendorf Reformatory was asked by fellow officials to give a short speech. He said this.

[All of the report is the spoken word. Speech quotes are omitted to keep the document simple]

GENTLEMEN, welcome to the Reformatory. Since there are but half-a-score of us, let us be as informal as we can. Discard your coats, you'll find hooks on the side walls. Chose a comfortable chair and draw nearer to the fire, for listening is hard when cold nags. Smoking is permitted. Hot toddy will be served after my short address and later our subject shall be thrown open for general comment.

You have asked me to talk about discipline, especially as it pertains to the young women in my charge. I have no need to remind you, any group of women in their late teens and early twenties, grouped together and living as closely as my charges do, can easily fall into bad habits. Girls by their nature can be petulant, sulky and throw a tantrum if they do not get their own way. Some may also be so foolish as to attempt to play the coquette, which leads to wilfulness and insolence. The phrase 'womanly conceit' was not coined by accident. To quell any rebellious nature and dampen unruliness and high spirits, I enforce strict discipline. If any young woman is less than polite, respectful and obedient I at once take the skin off her bottom.

It's the only way. If you're going to keep a girl obedient then she's got to know the meaning of a well-flogged bottom. I mean a bottom so sore she can't sit. I mean with welts that chafe and backs of the legs that hurt when the skirt rubs against them. No good talking to her, no good threatening to teach her a lesson, you've got to move in quick, seize her by the scruff, force the head down and lay on.

I don't spend time chastising them verbally. They know why I've called them out and they know they won't go back to their seat without a hole in the pit of their stomach and six burning welts cut across their tight arses. There's never the slightest chance that the culprit might be innocent and have been ordered to stand before me by mistake.

When the tickler starts to tap them behind the knees they know it's the start of a ritual. I question the miscreant about whether she has completed her work. She mumbles about being 'nearly done'. The tickler taps more urgently and slides up the back of her legs to beneath her skirt. The newcomers are the most fun because they begin to plead. Please, I'll try harder. Please, not today I'm in a fragile condition. Please, you thrashed me yesterday and I don't think I can bear another dose.

For a decade I've witnessed pleading, begging and wriggling to escape. There isn't an excuse any young woman can come up with that I haven't heard. I smile understandingly, shake my head and lower my eyes, I might even stop tapping the tickler. But any girl who has been in the 'house' for more than a fortnight knows that none of this sweet empathy means a damn.

Funny how differently they cry. With some the tears come with the first stroke. Others can take five or six before they break into song. What I specially like is when two or three give me a tune at the same time. They're not melodic but never mind that, their throats open, their eyes squeeze and out come the howls. With some it's snuffling and moaning, with others it's short sharp yelps of pain, with yet others it's a steady aaahh! with mouth open, eyes wet. Then there's the keening you get at wakes.

Oh I wake them alright; no sleeping when my tickler is busy. Rather they're high on their toes, jiggling and nimble with plenty of fancy footwork, heads thrown back, hair flying, chin up and the lips stretched in a yell. I don't mind how long that chorus goes on, I've had them at full throttle for ten minutes and whenever they look like quietening I'm in there like a ferret at a rabbit.

They never quite get used to it. Doesn't matter how often you call them out from the kitchen, laundry or scullery. The moment you chuck them under the chin with the point of the tickler they tremble with fright. Their eyes stare with that helpless look of fear and pleading. I tell them to stop making a fuss, pull themselves together, stop wringing that handkerchief, stand still with hands by their sides. Their eyes leak salt tears which cut a runnel down their soft, downy cheeks, sometimes running into their mouths. I've seen a tiny pink tongue dart out and capture a silver droplet before now and I've nodded to let the culprit know I've noticed and she'll take an extra three for the temerity.

It isn't true that every girl's bottom is noticeably different. Different categories I grant you. There are the trim tight ones that hardly protrude at all, almost boyish in their shape. There are slightly fuller ones, pleasantly rounded and firm enough to stand out. At the other extreme are the fat ones, not to my taste I'm afraid, although there are plenty I know who like a meaty rump to flog.

To me a big bottom is banal; rather my taste moves towards the other end of the scale. I like a girl with not too much flesh on her bones, with long legs and pert little cheeks, apple firm flesh and an apple-tight skin. A tight young bottom you may call a Cox's Pippin. And when the bottom is round, firm and suntanned the words Golden Delicious come to mind. Golden skin doesn't show the cane marks as vividly as the snow white flesh of a Granny Smith and I do like to be able to count every stroke of my efforts. But Golden Delicious, if it's topped with a narrow waist that leads upwards to champagne-glass tits has actually made me hold my hand and deliver only six cuts where a fat arse would certainly have got twelve.

What a difference between a girl who's never had the cane, and one who's getting a repeat dose. The former, not knowing what is in store, puts on a brave face and although she may not be impertinent or wish to question authority, she does not show that deep, fearsome respect that she should. When she bends it's with a mixture of courage and dignity and a belief that she will bear whatever she is given and try her best not to cry. Punishment is nasty, she thinks, but it cannot be so bad that she cannot bear it. She tells herself: 'I shall be strong, brave and fight to keep my dignity. If I am submissive when the caning is over it's only because I don't wish for more. But my spirit will still be my own, I will remain my own secret person and I will not be broken.'

All of which is tommyrot! It's foolishness and self-delusion. No amount of willpower can preserve a girl's composure and self-respect once the tickler gets busy. She may start feeling strong, but it takes only a few strokes before she is cowed and very few more before she understands the tickler is going to take her all the way to hell. And how could it be otherwise? The tickler never gets angry, feels no pain and knows nothing of pity or mercy.

From the moment the girl knows she is to be caned there begins a battle of wills, the will of a vulnerable, flesh-and-blood young woman against the will of a long whippy cane. The outcome is never in question and by the time we have finished her flesh is aflame and pulsing, her heart strumming, her eyes streaming and her will broken. And all this happens well before punishment is over. For even though I win every contest I enter, I still continue to cane to make the jackanapes pay for her insolence.

Compare opposition and defiance to a girl who has been thrashed before and has now to face further discipline. This young madam has an entirely different attitude for she knows she cannot win and her agonised buttocks will turn her into a dancing puppet, a demented doll performing a jig of torment, wheedling and beseeching to be spared. She cannot be spared, for to make any allowances would be to set a train of thought in motion which might lead to resurrection. My young women must know who is in command and what they must endure. If I express a whim they must race to satisfy it. If I issue a command they must obey with speed.

The alternative is to endure the tickler at his most persistent and go through an unholy ordeal. A second or third timer, as we may call her, hurries to her place, waits in terror and submits from the first stroke. This does not mean the tickler will be any the more lenient for as I say it has no feelings and is only hungry to complete its task. But if I see full submission and unfeigned remorse I can moderate punishment. Tears flow, of course, generally before the main business has begun, but it is sooner over and often the culprit, quite unbidden, will drop to her knees to beg forgiveness.

There are four punishment positions I use and for each the girl must be naked. If I am in the reception area, say, where there is no desk, no bed, and bare wooden floors, I will stand the unclothed girl upright, stretch her arms above her head and fasten her wrists to an upper beam, so she is on tip-toe. She can take the weight on the balls of her feet and stay balanced provided she is not touched.

When the tickler whistles across bare buttocks there is a tendency for her knees to bend so for a moment her feet may leave the floor. They touch down again quickly enough but balance is lost and if you cut at regular intervals she will dance and scrabble to stay grounded. Girls hung so can take up to a dozen but it is best not to keep them tied for too long as they may strain their under-arm muscles. When released from the shackles the wrists can be chafed and it is best to lead the girl to the wall to face the brickwork and let her hold herself upright. In due course two others can be delegated to help, and she will put her arms around their shoulders as they take her to the dormitory.

It will not surprise you to know the most-used position is to bend the girl over my desk, either with her arms stretched out sideways so she can grasp the desk-sides, or reaching across the desk-top so she can draw herself towards the opposite edge. I like the head turned away so she can neither see her punisher nor tell when the stripes are coming. Seeing the stripe as it is about to land cannot of course make it any less painful but it does allow the miscreant to prepare herself, perhaps stiffen her muscles and mentally grit her teeth. Kept completely ignorant of when the cane will fall creates a constant terror of being stroked even when the cane is at my side. It is a subtle thing but I do like to make punishment as terrible to contemplate and as hard to bear as I can.

The height of the desk is pre-ordained and designed to be sat behind, not bent over. But one has to decide whether the girl is allowed to stand with her feet flat on the floor or whether she should come away from the desk slightly and spread her legs wide so she goes up on her toes. On her toes the cut of the rod puts an extra strain on her legs, but it is of minor importance and if you cane hard enough it scarcely matters whether she's flat footed or on her points.

About the caning itself. You will have heard stories about Boys' Reformatories where usually there is a Sergeant at Arms to cane delinquents. The boy bends over a table and his tormentor is said to march to the end of the room, wind himself up like a tiger then rush forward and slice the boy's behind as though he is scything corn. I have to tell you that if any boy were caned that way, with such untrammelled ferocity they would be almost cut in half. More to the point the sabre-slash is not the most effective way to wield a stick.

What I find best is to use a cane some three-and-a-half feet long and carefully assess your distance from the presented bottom. Practice helps you take up your position quickly with the bottom within easy caning reach. Pull back the rod some little distance and by all means raise your arm slightly, but the swing need not be a long one, the pain is generated by adding a decisive twisting flick of the wrist at the moment of impact. It is no more complicated than that.

But you must flick hard, so you put real bite into the cut, flex the wrist muscles with all your strength, so it's not so much a cut from a great distance but a twisting stab with the length of the cane feeling like a thousand knife-points. Four or five of those and the most hardened culprit knows she is defeated and you will very soon have her pleading for leniency. I take no notice of such begging.

Rushing at the bottom and slashing wildly is an effective way to tell a juicy story but it by no means bears resemblance to real-life punishing. In life it would probably mean you miss the intended spot. You might also break the cane, do damage to the desk top and make a fool of yourself with your demonstrable lack of experience. Steady determination, the proper amount of concentration, a sense of occasion and the need to instil in the girl the seriousness of her offence are all more effective than an uncontrolled attack, however flamboyant a picture the latter may conjure up.

In the dormitory there are two positions the girl may assume, either touching her toes or lying face down on the bed. Of the two I find toe touching less efficacious since there is an almost irresistible temptation to swing upright the moment the rod strikes. You can (and I do) emphasise that every time the girl stands she earns herself a further stripe, but I find 'touch-your-toes' to be my least favourite position.

Flat on the bed is another matter. At first the girl is perhaps tempted to enjoy the tiniest release of tension for she is lying full length along the bed. I take several pillows and tuck them beneath her hips, so the buttocks are pushed well up and free from any encumbering blanket. The girl is then told to grasp the bed-head and hold on for dear life as I take my time measuring the distance, extending the waiting period, standing way out of sight of the recipient and generally contemplating what is always a pretty scene. The flogging when it comes can be hard and steady, there is no chance of the girl standing, slipping off the chair or desk, rubbing her buttocks or otherwise impeding punishment. You can go on slightly longer than you would if the girl were bent over and need not worry if the stripes are serious. The miscreant does not have to walk anywhere afterwards and can be left on the bed to cry herself to sleep and even stay resting until you decide she is ready to take up duties again.

The final position, and the one which is secretly my favourite, is where the girl is either on the bed, or on a desk top, flat on her back with her legs raised not just up in the air but bent over on themselves until the ankles are by her ears. This is difficult to achieve with a female who is tubby or worse, but for the girl with a lithe figure who has stayed supple through work, it is very effective. Ask me to choose between desk-top and mattress and I choose mattress for one simple reason. The girl's legs can be spread on a mattress so that her treasure is utterly disclosed. There is no way female charms can be hidden when the calves of her legs are alongside the cheeks of her face. Once those tender lips are vulnerable the girl's mind will do most of the work for you, for she will never be sure that you will resist the temptation to flog her *in there*.

When I have a girl heels over head I punish with the tawse. You can lay the tawse firmly across the backs of the thighs with relative impunity and prolong whipping much more than is advisable with a cane. The tawse metes out no less agony provided it is used well and if, as you come to the end of your session you decide that you will, if only once, admonish those tender inner lips, the tawse accomplishes that *coup de grace* better than the cane. I need not tell you that the memory of whipped inner lips stays with a girl for the rest of her life, the tale of my cruelty will be the talk of the dormitory and go down in legend as the most demonic act ever perpetrated.

Dormitory gossip is of course an essential part of my regime. The girls need no encouragement to talk about their chastisements and often those who have escaped the rod are anxious to see the effect it has had on those who have suffered. The girls may think I do not know of their unquenchable curiosity and believe if their inspections ever came to my attention I would forbid them. But I do know, and far from forbidding I relish its taking place, for it strikes awe and pity into everyone and encourages the company to reflect on how to avoid such suffering.

There is also, I suspect, a slightly more invidious side to seeing the results on someone who has been flogged severely. The observer thanks her maker that her own bottom is not so marked but she also – and I touch on this matter lightly since we are all gentlemen here – enjoys a strange and secret frisson of excitement at the whipping and might even experience certain palpitations in her (how shall I put it?) private regions. One thing I can tell you, if I am looking for a bottom to cane late at night, I will certainly find one if I go to a dormitory where a girl has been punished during the day, for by showing off her wounds she has excited several of her companions into a state where they cannot but pleasure themselves. And when I catch a girl in the throes of such self-abuse I rip the bedclothes off her, throw off her chemise, and have her heels over her head for a dozen quick cuts that soon put a stop to any pleasurable feelings she might be enjoying.

You will gather from what I have said neither cane or tawse lack employment in the Reformatory and it has to be so if the girls are to keep their home, clothes and bedding clean and attend to their chores. You may be surprised to learn half of them can scarce read or write and I must set that to rights before they are released. Any gentleman who would like to witness an everyday flogging please nod and I shall choose one of the girls and make an example of her here and now. They have been in bed a mere thirty minutes and it will not be the first time I've dragged a mischief-maker into wakefulness and put her to the test.

If you wish to forgo that experience, I thank you most sincerely for your courteous attention and throw our meeting open for questions. After questions we shall go straight into our debate. Ah… I see the toddy is on its way. I shall be grateful to soothe my throat after my address and for the moment, while we sample the refreshment, shall return to my seat. Thank you.

Goddess

Tulsa Brown

'PLEASE write down which issues you would like Madame to address today, Lieutenant,' Yu Chen Li said, handing me the familiar blank recipe card.

Her false fingernails were squared-off ovals, perfectly manicured to blunt ends that could never be confused with claws. They were painted gold, the only trace of glitz in the tiny Oriental woman's demure business attire. In the three years I'd been coming to Madame, I'd never heard Yu Chen raise her voice. We'd never talked about the traffic or the weather, not even in the midst of Montreal's worst blizzard.

Four women dead
Asphyxiated
500 meter radius of Notre-Dame Basilica
Angels?
Pregnancy alert bracelet

I crossed the last item off the list with three strokes. We hadn't concretely linked it to the case, nor posted it in the newspaper.

'May I have another card, please?' I asked.

Yu Chen smiled and dipped her head deferentially, the eternal geisha. 'You know the rules, Lieutenant.'

I did, dammit. Madame read these little cards like

Rorschach tests. My mistakes, the faintest tremble in the ink, were as important to her as the words I wrote. I sighed and handed the card back, my scribble glaring, neon nakedness: *Lieutenant Detective Dan Volka is uncertain and tentative today. His nuts are in knots.*

'Please take room number two, and Madame would like you to shave.'

I felt a clutch of alarm. 'I… can't. I'm playing racquetball this weekend. It's a tournament.'

Yu Chen raised an eyebrow, a roaring rebuke on her porcelain-smooth face. 'Madame canceled another appointment to make time for you. I thought this session was important, Lieutenant.'

It was – desperately. Something terrible was in process in the city, and my exhausted mind was a swamp, twisted, gnarled roots and bottomless mud. For more days than I cared to remember, I'd been running in relentless circles, chasing specters of leads, or gnawing the same clues until they were shapeless nubs. Then yesterday afternoon, another body had been discovered, and the swamp had become a maelstrom. At 8pm I'd phoned Yu Chen to beg for an appointment.

'Madame is very gracious,' I said. I relinquished my credit card, feeling the usual small gust of relief that there was no one who would question the charge. I left the reception area and set out into the process.

Inside room two, I waited as the heavy door eased shut behind me, the decisive, metallic clink of the bolt vibrating in my bones. It was locked now. The only way out was through the other door on the opposite wall, just as plain as the one I'd entered by, except for the four explicit words above the frame: *You have chosen this.*

The only way out was through Madame.

The room was Spartan: a tub and shower, toilet, sink and mirror, one padded bench. The unscented soap and shampoo were always the same. The only alterations came in the hygiene products Madame might select for the day. The enema equipment had terrified me at first, but I didn't see it often. Today's extras were the shaving cream and disposable razor.

No racquetball tournament for Dan Volka. I couldn't imagine running around on the court with shaved skin, my winter-white legs stark and strange despite the muscles. The other players were from the force, too, men I'd known for ten and fifteen years. All in our forties, we were called the geezer league by the young bucks, but we were ferocious competitors and the best of friends.

No one knew I came to a place like this.

I turned on the water and set the temperature with precise movements, as regimented as the gestures of Tai Chi. I placed the towels in neat, folded squares on the floor, always the same way now. It had taken me a year to fully appreciate Madame's words: 'Ritual is not simply repetition. It is powerful preparation.'

She was right, of course. I unzipped my pants and my cock was already swelling, lengthening, tingles licking the base of my balls. At the same time, my heart thudded with apprehension, but fear wouldn't stop this process now, or pain. I'd come to Madame for something more important than those two trifles.

Focus.

I used to play chess, played it with the total absorption of the addicted, rushing on the consuming high of concentration and mental battle. Until the age of thirty-nine, I ran, too, competing in local marathons, even though I didn't have a runner's body. I was fit but bulky, bones too dense, shoulders too broad, an animal designed to fight, not flee.

That meant every day's training was penance, and the events themselves were grueling ordeals, stomach cramping, muscles howling. I ran anyway, hating the pain and reveling in my hatred, how it cleared the stubble and sharpened my mind to a laser point. When I finally thrashed my dead husk body across the fiery finish, my thoughts could have cut granite.

'You masochist!' my friend Andre LeFavre laughed. 'Go to the gym. Or better yet, pay me. Hell, I'd pound on you for a couple of hours a day.'

I didn't need chess or marathons anymore.

After the shower, I allowed three inches to accumulate in the tub, then crouched on my knees. I was fully erect and trembling with trepidation, and excitement. A maddening little imp masquerading as logic jabbered on my shoulder.

People are dying, and you're shaving yourself like a Hollywood whore? You're paying two days' salary to get your rocks off, Volka?

Focus. I lathered the foam over my chest and began shaving in short downward strokes, carefully circumventing my nipples.

The first time Madame had arranged for this had been my fourth visit. For three sessions she'd just explored me, my physical needs and limits, tentatively probed the psyche I clung to, and thought I hid. Then abruptly she'd turned the key in the lock.

'Ross will shave you now,' Madame said.

And he did, with a straight razor. I stood in a tub of

ankle-deep water, clinging with both hands to a metal ring above my head, and watched my video image projected on the wall: a pale, strapping forty year old man under a spotlight, being lathered and scraped by a black bodybuilder in a thong. Ross was oiled and he gleamed; his single, dangerous blade flashed when it caught the light. I was very hard, dick and balls harnessed in a leather cock-ring, throbbing at the edge of pain. It was hypnotic, terrifying.

'Spread,' Ross said.

I widened my stance as far as the tub would allow, his touch rippling through me in gusts of alarm. I held my breath as his deft hands lathered me behind my balls, and up the crack of my ass. Even with his handling, the blade was cold, a long, dangerous weapon that rasped as it sheared the short, protective curls away. I clenched the ring above me, and narrowed all my powers of concentration into a single command: *Don't move.*

Then Madame's voice floated out of the darkness, a diaphanous scarf trailing leisurely on a breeze.

'We've never spoken about your work, Lieutenant.'

I flinched and Ross swore; I never felt the cut. My heart pounded, knowing that my weaknesses were laid upon her plate now. She understood why I was here. And my title, the polished rail of rank that held others back, was a call to her. She curled the word with the lightest flip of her French tongue, nailed it for the grand joke it was.

'Madame, we must stop,' Ross said. 'He's bleeding.'

'What a pity to pause when we have finally begun,' Madame said thoughtfully, but the unbreakable rule about blood was her own.

That was three years ago. I still had the scar, a faint

line high on my inner thigh that only the most devoted lover would notice. It hadn't been a problem.

I was truly naked by the time I dried off, every pass of the towel sending fresh sensation over my body, down my legs, around my genitals, whispering up between my buttocks. I felt light and anxious, a runner in the starting block, heart thrumming with desire and dread. I paused in front of the door, reading the words once more.

Don't forget you've chosen this, Dan Volka.

The room was about twenty-five feet square, although it was difficult to be certain. Only the pertinent parts were illuminated at any one moment, by spotlights or video images projected on the wall. The darkened ceiling was a jungle of cords, metal lamps and cameras – the machinery behind the magic. I knew Madame used a handheld remote but it seemed incomprehensible that she could orchestrate a light and sound show, and perform on a man at the same time. I suspected that Ross had more duties than I knew about.

He was waiting for me now, arms folded like a huge mahogany sentry as he stood beside the stark beam that illuminated the black sponge mat. Two manacles dangled from chains and I prayed Ross's only job was to help me into them; when he fucked me I was crippled for days.

A single red circle was projected on the wall. It began as a fierce dot, no more than a cigarette tip, that expanded and diffused until it was a warm glow, the size of a dinner plate. Then it contracted into a dot again. It was a rhythmic throb of light, accompanied by a perfectly-timed pulsing hum. Open and close, open and close.

I walked obediently to the mat, but when Ross lifted my arms, I felt the gut-wrench of instinct to pull away, run before it was too late. I took a deep breath and held myself still, and he closed the cuffs around one wrist, then the other. The restraint spread me into a Y, my pectoral muscles tingling, taut.

Ross glanced up and down my shaved body, and smirked. For an awful second I thought he was going to reach between my legs and touch the scar, but he bent in a mocking little bow and backed into the darkness.

The room was very warm. I waited, anticipation clenching in my belly like a fist. To calm myself I focused on the pulsating light, counted five rotations, then ten. Its simple hypnotic pattern seemed to draw me into its center, called to engulf me. Is this how sperm saw the ova? I wondered.

Then click-snap, click-snap. My erection bobbed. Madame had entered the room behind me, and she was wearing mules. I listened to her unhurried progress across the hardwood, the distinct strike of the sole, then the tantalizing smack against her heel. It almost sounded wet, and I thought longingly of the time she'd let me lick her feet.

'Today we are going to talk about time, Lieutenant,' Madame said. Her English was perfect, but there was a slant to the words, if not exactly an accent. She was fullbred Quebecois, and kept that edge of herself polished to a gloss. 'How long does it take to be strangled?'

A breath of winter swept over me. There would be no preliminaries. 'Four minutes, or five.'

'And when I whip you with a crop, how long does that take?'

Oh, God – forever. It felt like an eternity. 'I don't know.'

She was very close to my back. I felt a flutter against

my inner thigh and flinched, but she was only stroking me with the leather, exploring the newly-bare skin. The throbbing dot on the wall disappeared, replaced by a video of a woman's leg, an extreme close-up that followed the smooth skin up to a tight triangle of black pubic hair. The thrill surged to my cockhead in a rush of blood; it felt like a club swaying between my legs.

The tip of Madame's lash traced the cleft of my ass.
'*Why* don't you know, Lieutenant?'

On the wall, the video woman spread her legs wider, and began to tease her rosy vagina lips with the end of a riding crop. The cuffs bit into my wrists as I strained forward, but experience was crying alarm. *For God's sake, answer her, Dan.*

'Because I am…'

Crack! A welt of pain seared my left buttock and I wrenched, the manacle chains squeaking at the ceiling bolt.

'Easily distracted, Lieutenant?'
'Yes, Madame,' I gasped. *Fuck, that hurt.*
'That's why we are going to play with time – to help you concentrate. I will ask questions and you will answer them, within two seconds. Right or wrong, I don't care. Guess if you have to, but you *will* answer. You will not say *I don't know.*'

On the wall, the woman's sex glistened. She lifted her hips in a slow undulation, rubbing against the crop as if it were a braided leather pole, the way a stripper would. I knew I would concentrate better if I didn't watch, so I closed my eyes. I opened them again immediately. Addict.

'How old were the girls who were murdered?'
'Two were fifteen, one eighteen, one sixteen.'

'Prostitutes?'

'One.'

'How do bikers dispatch their enemies, Lieutenant?'

The question caught me off guard and I hesitated, mentally running through the dozen gang murders in the last year.

Crack! The savage bite of the whip made me twist, half in pain, half in animal fury.

'They shoot them, Madame! Car bombs, knifings.'

'Then why do you waste your time on the Hell's Angels?'

'Because they're at war with Les Bandits, over teen hookers. Did you read in *La Presse*…'

One blow, then another, stinging nettles across each thigh. *God damn!*

'I'm the one asking the questions, Lieutenant.'

It went on and on, eternity creeping forward in two-second increments, the distance between her question and the lash. My ass danced and my mind scrambled ahead in a ragged, desperate dash. I quickly exhausted my own logical theories and reached for wild conjecture: truth, guesses, bald lies – I tossed out anything to save my skin.

Yet she caught me again and again, and always with the same bait. On the wall, the first woman was replaced by two others, who were joined together, feasting between each other's thighs. I was mesmerized by the undulating landscapes, one pale and one caramel, ass cheeks bucking in slow, sinuous waves, breasts trembling with soft weight. My erection had dipped but now it surged again, straining forward eagerly. I ached to touch it.

'Which girl was pregnant?'

'Neither...' They were two tigresses lapping cream, I thought, then caught myself. 'None!' I blurted. Oh, God, she'd read through my scribble on the card.

'You expect your superiors to have faith in an officer who is so uncertain, *Lieutenant*?' She squashed the word like a grape under her heel. 'Do you waste their time like you waste mine?'

I thought the question was rhetorical. The vicious blow caught me under the shoulder blades and I cried out, a curse of rage and pain.

'Who did the bracelet belong to?' Madame demanded.

'No one – I don't know. Not the killer!'

'Why not? Explain.'

I did, feeling guilty for my breach – that information hadn't been released to the public. But I was grateful for any kind of respite.

The bracelet had been found at the scene with the first body, and while it was being held as a clue, it could have been dropped at any time, by anyone. Notre-Dame Basilica was very popular with both tourists and the faithful. Our department didn't believe it was the perpetrator's because female serial killers were very, very rare. Most were poisoners; these strangulations had been brutal, hands-on murders. We had no record of violent serial killings being committed by a pregnant woman.

The video image on the wall changed again. This one was a shock. It took me moments to recognize it, that pale, trembling body stretched between chains, torso bowed, shaved skin gleaming with sweat.

You chose this, Dan Volka. Oh, God.

Then Madame slipped out of the darkness and pressed her leather-clad body against the length of my ravaged back. I could have brayed in anguish but I swallowed it back to a low, whimpering moan in my throat. Madame laid her cheek between my shoulder blades, reached around my hips and began to caress my flagging erection with glistening, grease-smeared hands.

Extreme close-up. Extreme bliss. My cock on the wall was two feet long and her delicate, feminine hands slithered over it, coaxing urgent life into it once more. She stroked the base, and the virgin skin tingled with fresh excitement, shimmering waves that lapped over my balls. Her other hand slid up and down the hardening shaft, smeared pre-cum over the throbbing head, stroked the cleft with her thumb. It was glorious, a sensual, serpentine dance that was intensified by its own image, a porno flick I saw *and* felt.

'Daniel,' she murmured against my back, 'why did I ask you to shave?'

The tenderness in her voice caught me by surprise, and my throat tightened. 'To humiliate me,' I whispered.

'No.' She closed her thumb and forefinger in a ring under my cockhead, and squeezed. I groaned at the video image, the immense, dark-rose cap that seemed to be sitting on her fist, and the surge of sensation that churned between my legs.

'I wanted you to remember places you had forgotten,' she said. 'I wanted you to feel them new, to begin again.' Pause. 'I do read *La Presse*, Lieutenant, and most of the other papers, too. I've been expecting you for a week. I read the headlines and I know the pressure you're under, I can feel the disorder of your thoughts.'

She released me and stepped away. I almost cried out at the loss. But she set a little step in front of me, slipped out of her mules and got up on it. Her eyes were level with mine, and I stared into her face, startled and amazed by this unexpected privilege. This was Madame facing me like a lover, not bits of anatomy flickering on the wall.

She was forty, certainly. No woman, no matter how beautiful, could have gathered that power of presence in twenty years, or even thirty. Her cheekbones were high and defined, her dark hair was still glossy, dyed, perhaps, and pulled back severely into a chignon. There was a delicate line on each side of her mouth, the tug of gravity on fine flesh, and a soft feathering of time at the edges of her eyes. But her dark gaze was alert, penetrating. A falcon.

She smelled of leather, and roses. She clasped my face with both hands.

'Do you doubt the capacity of a woman to be terrible, Lieutenant?'

No.

'I will tell you, I was pregnant once,' she continued quietly. 'Twenty years ago. They call it the miracle of life, and it was – the miracle of mine. The power of creation was in my body. What other powers might I have? It was the beginning of a new journey. Some women become mothers, and a few become... goddesses.'

I was transfixed, held by her hands and her glittering eyes. What she was suggesting was ludicrous – that the ability to produce new life might lead someone to believe she could dole out death, too? Yet, in the back of my mind, I heard the hum of the red light again, saw its timeless, repeating, consuming pulse.

'Think again, Daniel,' Madame whispered. 'Start at the beginning and do not doubt what a woman may be capable of, upon your peril.'

She pulled me forward into a kiss, and clamped my cock between her powerful thighs. That sensation eclipsed all others, pushed pain and exhaustion into the surreal past. I was embraced by tight heat, soaring in the sudden rush, overwhelmed by it. Greased and ready, I began to buck into the warm clasp of her flesh. In that instant I loved it like no other.

Madame closed her fists in my hair, hanging on as I thrust my hips in wild, needy lunges, terrified she would pull away again. I drove harder, faster until I was shaking her, my chains holding us both. I heard a raw sound, an animal in the distance – it was myself moaning. I climbed and climbed, numb to everything now except that pinnacle I wanted so desperately to reach.

Rapture. I convulsed, twisted by pleasure so sharp it began as pain, a thunderclap roaring up from my balls. All the tortured waiting, teasing, misery and urgent hunger spun together in a white sphere and released, shooting deep into the blackness beyond her thighs.

I sagged, trembling. Madame unlocked my cuffs and I fell to my knees. My arms were dead wood except for the grinding ache in the sockets; I couldn't raise them. My swollen hands were throbbing mitts, my legs, rubber. I leaned forward until my forehead touched the mat.

'Au revoir, Lieutenant,' Madame said. I heard her slip into her mules and walk away, the distinct steps on the hardwood ringing throughout the room. Click-snap, click-snap, faster now.

I lay there, a crumpled, battered man, still shuddering

with pleasure. I couldn't move yet but the gift from my goddess was already in motion, burning ahead of me, the clear, white beacon of my thoughts.

It lit up the tiniest stone, a pebble of possibility that cast a very long shadow. Twenty years long. I pushed myself up on one arm, ignoring the scream in my shoulder.

'Did you have a son – or a daughter?' I called out.

Madame turned at the open door, a thrilling magazine fantasy with dangerous white legs and a fine, high-breasted body, armored in black leather. But the face above it floated, a tremulous petal in a pond. I realized I'd never seen her look afraid.

Way Out West

Suzee Moon and Stan Strap

STAN shook some dust from his red bandana and tied it loosely at his neck before pushing open the swing doors of The Lucky Seven. It was nine o' clock on a summer's night in Tombstone and the place was packed. Old George was belting out *Beautiful Dreamer* on the slightly out of tune piano, and, best of all, Stan noticed Miss Kitty and her girls were already mingling with the crowd.

There was the usual pause as when anyone stepped in, but most people knew Stan and those who didn't were quickly advised to leave him be. When he ordered his usual drink of sarsaparilla no one laughed. For one thing he was the only one who could spell it, and for another they remembered the night that Scruffy Jake had made fun of him. The memory of what followed still made hard men wince.

A big bear of a man standing next to him at the bar turned and said, 'You gonna let me take your money off you in poker tonight, Deputy?'

'The hell I will, Calhoun,' said Stan. 'You know I never play cards.'

'Just checking,' said Calhoun with a chuckle, 'you

know where I'm sitting if you want to join us.' He nodded to the far corner.

'You take care now,' said Stan.

He took his drink and went to sit near the piano.

'What'll it be, Stan?' Old George asked him.

'I've been out in the desert for three days. Play me some music with rocks in it.'

George began a rolling left hand pattern and then added triplets across the beat with his right.

'That's fine,' said Stan tapping his boots, 'just fine.'

After a while, Miss Kitty came over to see him. 'You looking for company tonight?' she asked him.

As it happened one of the girls had caught Stan's attention. It was the tumbling black hair that had first attracted him, quickly followed by the full curve of her delightful hips. When he noticed the sassy look in her eyes, he just knew he had to have her.

As it happened Stan had caught the girl's attention, too. Tales of the deputy had filtered through the saloon and he was preceded by his reputation. Good lovers were not exactly common in the back-of-beyond, but nor were they that thick on the ground in Kansas. It was not that which had intrigued Suzee, though. It was the rumour of his delight at upturning a pretty woman's bottom for a sound spanking that had caused her to shiver, despite her show of contemptuous outrage when one of the girls had warned her to behave herself in front of the deputy. No one was going to tell Suzee what to do! She'd had enough of men trying to rule her life in Kansas. Here she was going to be a big fish in a little bowl, she'd decided. As a dancer she'd never made it further than the chorus line in Kansas, but here at The Lucky Seven she could be a star.

Suzee was a natural flirt and as a dancer and hostess she knew how to perform but was usually sensible not to push things too far. She didn't believe flirting entitled anyone to her favours, but she knew that with so few women around it was easy to stir up a situation that could turn nasty. So why the heck did she suddenly turn up the flame as soon as she sensed the legendary deputy's presence? Of course it was nothing to do with Deputy Strap's entrance, or the rumours she'd heard...

'Who's that?' the deputy asked, pointing to Suzee who was now bent so low that her ample breasts looked in real danger of tumbling out of her low cut gown. And did she actually push down her dress further as she pretended to rearrange her hair? Stan didn't know whether to be outraged or amused, but the stirring in his constraining denim was unambiguous in its appreciation of the hussy. Stan couldn't help stare with baited breath, unaware that clever corsetry allowed Suzee to flash outrageously with no danger of escape. Those almost tumbling assets of hers made the mesmerised Stan long to uncover her more modestly covered assets and give her the spanking she undoubtedly deserved.

Stan sighed to himself. Much as he longed to have her over his knee, she was new to town, and perhaps was not as worldly as she appeared. True, her dress seemed tighter and lower cut than some of the other girls' frocks but she was from Kansas. A word of advice would be more appropriate, he decided reluctantly...

His reverie was broken by Kitty's contemptuous response: 'That's the new girl, Suzee. She's fresh in from Kansas City and she's driving the guys wild.'

'I can see why,' said Stan as he watched her flirt and sway from one table to another. 'Call her over.'

Kitty looked unsure. 'The thing is, Stan, she's new to the work. She sees herself as a dancer and hostess only, if you take my meaning.'

'That would be fair enough if she wasn't going around swaying that lovely behind of hers, and bending over the table in that low-cut bodice. Don't worry Kitty. I just want a word. She needs to behave herself if she's not for sale. And when have I ever gone where I wasn't invited?' he smiled at her. 'Or paid for it?' he added giving her rump a lazy slap as he grinned at her.

Kitty blushed, despite herself. 'I know, Stan. She is a terrible tease.'

'Call her over,' said Stan. 'She won't tease me for too long.'

Suzee had watched the exchange between Kitty and Stan in excitement and contempt. She noted the sly smack that had caused Kitty to turn quite girlish. There was no way Suzee would let any man treat her with such casual contempt and get away with it. And how dare he pay Kitty such attention when she was in the room! Had the man no taste? She felt a flicker of triumph when Kitty told her that the deputy wanted a word. Suzee took great delight in choosing her words. The fear and excitement she was trying so hard to contain were not assuaged by the look of amazement, nor the sly grin Kitty gave as Suzee delivered her message.

A minute later Kitty returned. She seemed unsure whether to laugh or run for cover.

'She says she's busy for a moment but she'll be over as soon as she has time.'

'Will she now?'

Stan stood up slowly and moved languidly across the room. He came up close to Suzee as she joked with Gil Calhoun while sitting on his knee.

'Excuse me,' he said, putting his hand very lightly on her wrist. 'Can I have a word with you for a moment?'

'If you don't mind,' said Suzee haughtily 'I'll see you when I'm through here.'

Everyone around the table took a sudden interest in their shoes. There was a long pause during which the silence began to spread to the next table.

'That's okay,' said Calhoun suddenly grinning. 'You go and chat with the Deputy while I finish my card game.'

Suzee looked affronted as Calhoun roughly pushed her from his lap but before she could say too much about it, Stan led her over to his seat near the piano.

'Well, really,' Suzee sniffed and tossed her head, 'what a terrible display of manners. I would have thought that as lawman you would be setting a better example.'

'It is partly because I am a lawman that I want to speak to you. You're not helping me to keep good order if you're going to flaunt yourself at the men and then turn them down if they get too frisky.'

'Who says I'm flaunting?' She crossed her legs revealing tight black ankle boots with three-inch heels. 'Or turning anyone down?' she added, dangerously.

Stan realised that he was staring at her. Damn but she was a bewitching woman. He took in the full breasts and deep cleavage and the way her skirt sat across her thighs. He decided to show her a very good example.

'So what's the problem anyway?' she asked him

insolently. 'Everybody knows I'm just playing. There's no law against it for heaven's sake.'

'There is if I decide there is,' said Stan.

'Oh yes,' said Suzee looking straight into his eyes. 'I bet you just want to get me into that jail of yours and put the handcuffs on me.'

'No,' said Stan. 'The punishment for breaking this law is a full spanking.'

Suzee laughed out loud, hoping he wouldn't be aware of her wildly beating heart as she struggled to sound amused and unbelieving. 'I haven't been spanked since I was a child. Now that I'm a full grown woman I don't think it would be very appropriate, do you?' and Suzee told herself it was pure thoughtlessness that made her add 'Besides I hardly think you're man enough…'

Any hesitation or doubt was crushed as soon as Suzee uttered those fatal words. Whatever she tried to tell herself, Suzee and Stan knew that the gauntlet had been thrown down and the die cast. They both knew that despite any protests Suzee had sealed her own fate.

'Yes, I think it would be very appropriate,' said Stan, catching her wrist again as she made to stand up.

'This is quite ridiculous,' she started to say but Stan was having none of it and quickly had her over his knee with her arm held behind her back.

'Give me some music I can beat time to,' he said to George who obliged with *The Band Played On* as Stan began to slap her ample backside in waltz time. People on tables nearby started to laugh and a couple of the girls drifted over.

Despite her fantasies and thoughts of the deputy, who she had been imagining since the first rumours she'd heard, Suzee did not enjoy the laughter. In her imagination such an event would be strictly private, not witnessed by the pig-ignorant staff and patrons of Hicksville. She was a contrary woman, and although she knew she'd given the deputy no choice (and of course she knew he was dying to spank her!) she felt humiliated and couldn't help her struggling and avoidance. At some unacknowledged level Suzee also felt disappointed that her first spanking was making so little impression... Of course she didn't want to be in pain... did she?

'She's never going to feel much under that skirt,' Kitty said. 'Let me lift it up so you can really get through to her.'

As more laughter started and a few more gathered round, Kitty said 'I know what you girls are like in this hot weather. I just hope you remembered to put your drawers on today, Suzee.' Despite Suzee's howls of protest and though she struggled furiously, Stan held her firm while Kitty raised her skirts. Suzee was genuinely horrified at the thought of her exposure, but she couldn't help herself thinking about the desire her exposed boots, stockings and drawers would arouse in the men and especially in the deputy...

Some of the men were disappointed to find that she had remembered after all but Stan was secretly thrilled to see the thin white cotton stretched over her plump cheeks. He had already decided that the pleasure of removal of those drawers was a joy to come. The only question would be who would take them down, her or him... He began to slap each cheek hard, over and over, until her squealing turned to yelling and she called him a whole bunch of names she surely couldn't have learned in Kansas City. And though she kicked her legs and wriggled like crazy, he kept up an insistent rhythm that he knew must be reddening her entire bottom.

When he paused for a moment with Suzee still squirming and complaining on his lap, Kitty said, 'I don't think she is learning her lesson. I think we'll have those drawers undone. See how she likes it on the bare.'

There were whoops from the men and Suzee gave a scream trying even harder to wriggle away but just as Kitty was reaching for the bow at the waistband, Stan stopped her and said 'Just hang on there a minute, Miss Kitty.'

He whispered something into Suzee's ear and after a second or two he smiled as she nodded her head and stopped struggling.

'I'm sorry folks,' he said, helping her to stand and then standing himself. 'Some things are better done in private.'

There were some murmurs of disapproval but not too many and not too loud. Miss Kitty though looked particularly put out.

'Well you make sure she learns her lesson,' she said crossly.

Stan looked at her. 'Surely you haven't forgotten how thorough my lessons can be?'

'No, Deputy, I haven't,' she said suddenly averting her eyes. She rubbed her bottom at the memory of the sting of Stan's hands on her tender skin.

'Well then…'

Suzee who had read between the lines did not miss the look or its meaning.

'Take her up to room six. It will be free all night.'

'Thanks,' said Stan as he took Suzee by the hand and led her upstairs. The piano was rolling again and the noise level in the room had returned to raucous.

Suzee's head was reeling as the deputy politely but firmly marched her up the stairs and into the room. She knew that with Kitty baying for her blood and her gentlemen 'admirers' aroused, a trip back downstairs would end in total humiliation. True, she'd often wondered about having her drawers taken down for a public spanking, but reality, she was discovering, was a little different. Her bottom was really stinging. Suzee knew she had an agreement with the lawman, but she couldn't help trying to talk herself out of it. She found herself rather drawn to speculation about the ominous bulge in the deputy's jeans and told herself she must be feeling sexy because of the flirting. There was no way Suzee was ready to admit even to herself, how sexy her first trip over a man's knee had been.

Suzee tried to hide the tremble she felt in her voice, thighs and breasts. She drew herself up on her slender heeled boots, tossed her hair and did her best to meet his quizzical stare. He surely wasn't *amused* by her?

'You don't really want to spank me any more, do you?' said Suzee very quietly and seductively. Stan locked the door behind them and hung his gun belt on the hook. He turned to admire her for a moment but much as he would like to lose himself in the fullness of her curves, he forced himself to wait.

'Surely you can think of something you'd rather do?' she said in a low sexy, drawl.

'Maybe later,' said Stan forcing himself to be brusque. 'First of all let's have those skirts and petticoats off.

Suzee could not believe her ears. Perhaps the oaf hadn't realised what she was offering him.

'I'm a grown woman, alone in a bedroom with you. You've been rather... rude, but I'm willing to overlook it if you apologise nicely...' She forced herself to smile at him; 'Now what can I do for you, Deputy?' she drawled.

Stan grinned at her.

'Sweetheart the only decision will be whether I have you on your knees or bent over that bed when I fuck you. There's nothing like the sight of a well-striped bottom to spur a man on...'

He *was* laughing at her, the bastard. Suzee knew there was no escape from that room but she hadn't given up.

She did as she was told but Stan could see that she was still hoping to entice him as she slowly stripped down to her bodice, drawers and boots. Who'd have thought that fancy frock would have so many buttons, hooks and ribbons, he wondered. He was used to feminine paraphernalia, but never had a woman taken so long to step out of her dress for the deputy. Much as he enjoyed the show, he knew Suzee was earning herself a little extra in both the spanking and fucking department. She was a vision. Despite his eagerness for the back view, her restricted but displayed breasts rising out of her tight white bodice caused a twitch in Stan's denims. Her knee-length, thin white drawers hinted at further delights, above her little boots and dark stockings.

'Now take hold of the edge of the bed.'

'What? Like this?' She stood near the edge of the brass bed and wiggled her backside.

'Take a step or two back, but don't let go.'

Suzee did as he asked and then gave another little wriggle.

Yup! The back view was worth waiting for! He could make out the tops of her stockings and garters under the now tightened white drawers, as well as detect the pinkness of her bottom under the thin stretched material. Gorgeous as she looked, there was no way the minx was going to keep her drawers up. Stan was torn. Did he want Suzee's first bare-bottomed spanking to be with those drawers rudely parted so they framed her naughty soon-to-be-striped bum or should he lower them to her thighs? On the other hand, he reasoned, if he removed them entirely he'd get to see her thighs and reddening behind nicely contrasted with those dark stockings and frilly garters…

Stan made up his mind and stepped forward. 'And we'll just untie these,' he said reaching for the bow and then releasing her pink cheeks from their confines under the cotton. He'd decided to part her drawers so that her bottom was rudely displayed, but surrounded by the snowy white of her drawers. He noted the slight pink of his earlier ministrations with some satisfaction.

Suzee couldn't believe the brute was really going to spank her! Her instincts had told her he would and part of her admired his determination, but now she was really worried. Never had anyone dared to treat Suzee like this and now she was bent over with her bared backside displayed for his attentions. She knew that the privacy of the room was a consideration for which she should be grateful, but Suzee was feeling anything but grateful as she felt her drawers expertly parted.

He could not resist stroking and squeezing her

delicious bottom before catching himself in time and giving her a series of hard slaps. Once Suzee knew there was no way out she concentrated on trying not to cry out but it was hard. He was pleased when he started to get through to her and she began to give little cries and sucked in the air between her teeth.

Not until he was satisfied that her bum was blazing did he stop for a moment.

Suzee let out a long breath and relaxed. 'I think I've learned my lesson,' she said beginning to stand up only to have Stan place her firmly back in position.

'Your lesson is by no means over.'

'But I'm really burning. I won't be able to take much more.'

When he started to unbuckle his belt she turned at the sound of it. 'What...'

'This belt was given to me by an Apache chief. He used one just like it to keep his wives in order.'

'I'm not having some savage's belt across my backside like this.'

'True,' said Stan, pulling her drawers down to her ankles. 'You are taking it like this.'

'I won't, I don't think... Aaaiiieee!'

Stan had landed a good stroke right across the centre of her hot cheeks. Suzee jumped up clutching herself. 'No, I can't take that. Don't ask me to.'

'You can have it downstairs in the bar if you'd prefer.'

'No, no,' said Suzee quickly, bending over and clutching the bedpost for dear life. 'How many must I have?'

'I'm not sure yet. See how we go. But one thing I am sure of: if you leap up like that we start over.'

He let her wait and sway and tremble for a moment

before landing a full swing that sounded like a gunshot.

Suzee screamed and jumped up again. 'It's no good I can't take that.'

'It's either this here. Or bare over the piano stool.'

'Not downstairs, no. But I can't stay down for it. I know I've got to take my spanking but you'll have to help me.' Suzee, bum blazing, was no longer playing with the deputy. With tears in her eyes, she accepted his authority as she desperately rubbed her throbbing cheeks. Stan's heart softened and his straining cock stiffened, but Suzee had a lesson to learn and Stan had every intention of taking his pleasure fully. He also knew that if Suzee wasn't thoroughly spanked, both of them would regret it, no matter how much she pleaded.

Stan reached for his gun belt at the door. Right behind the holster were the silver-plated handcuffs he always carried. He heard Suzee's sharp intake of breath and unconscious little moan. He hadn't forgotten it was Suzee who'd first mentioned handcuffs. And he knew that this inexperienced woman was having genuine difficulty in staying in position for the belt she had reluctantly agreed to take. Quickly, he put her wrists through the bars of the bedstead and handcuffed them in place.

Suzee hung her head and waited. He could see her knees trembling and watched with fascination as her whole bottom seemed to clench and then quiver as she waiting for the strokes to fall. This time he did not swing with full force but rather directed stinging swipes to each burning cheek in turn. Suzee hopped and swayed but there was no escape and Stan did not stop again until he had striped her poor bum twice. Finally, he reverted to full force and laid four dreadful stripes across both cheeks at once.

As the echo of the last swipe died in the room, Stan released the sobbing woman from the handcuffs and held her while she recovered. After a while she said 'I have learned my lesson now.'

Stan wiped her tear-stained face with a gentle finger.

'I'm sure you have. Do you want time to dress?'

Suzee shook her head. Instead of pulling up her drawers, she stepped out of them.

Stan drew her to him. They kissed. It was the first of many…

A New Understanding

Pearl Jones

'I'D like to ask you something.' His breath was hot and moist against my breast, his frame lying stickily on mine as we panted in the wake of pleasure. I wasn't ready for words but made some sort of sound, enough to encourage him to continue.

He did, but not with speech. His hand pressed between us and he shifted to the side, winding his fingers into my pubic hair. Gripping tight, he pulled and my body followed, pelvis arching upward. I gasped, my heart raced.

He'd done this before, a time or two, and I'd been amazed at the sensation: pain, but not pain. A heightened sense of pleasure. It had shocked me that first time, and I'd tried hard not to think about it after, determined just to be grateful that he knew so well how to please me. The time he'd used his mouth and that grip, I'd had the only screaming orgasm of my life, and though we'd just parted, I was suddenly eager for him again.

'Tell me,' he breathed, and licked my nipple. Words? I couldn't think to speak! I moaned; he laughed and sucked my flesh into his mouth. Arched to meet his attentions, I quivered and pled. I don't know what I managed to stammer, but something sufficed. He freed his mouth, making me groan in dismay. 'I think it's time you did me a favor. What do you say?' And all the time his fingers tugged and pushed.

'Anything,' I panted, as one finger crept low, finding my clitoris easily. He brushed his nail very gently over the hood, which made me writhe. A more serious caress followed, and I think I briefly lost my mind, too desperate to come to consider, to care, to breathe. He obliged my need, slicking fingers on either side of my clit, pinching and twisting and stroking, his other hand thrusting inward and up, hard, until I came.

Until the world ceased in its turning. Oh, I hate words. I can never manage to make them mean the right things. Look, usually when I come it's like my clit exploded. All the writhing and stroking freezes for a second, and then I shatter into bits. There's this great feeling of being thrown away from my body, and then my muscles all release and I come to rest. Sometimes I see lights behind my eyes, I've even lost my hearing. Like dying, only joy instead of pain. This time, it wasn't like that at all.

The focus was different. It came from deep inside me and washed out like waves, as if I were an ocean. There was no freezing feeling, no shattering; I felt suspended in mid-air. Not like I'd escaped my body, but more like my body had stopped existing in time. Nothing moved around me that I could feel, or hear, or sense. I was the only being anywhere. It was incredible. Unlike anything I'd felt before.

A single eternal instant. And then it faded away, and I lay half beneath my lover, wreathed in smiles. He curled himself around me, preparing for sleep; I murmured something affectionate and leaned into his arms.

'Do you remember what you said?' His voice was a whisper, but even so, I could hear the satisfied purr.

I remembered, but couldn't be bothered to worry. 'Anything,' I sighed, and fell asleep.

Ooh, what Sarah would say about this! I'm a high school teacher, mathematics and physics. Sarah is my best friend; she teaches English. And she would have dragged out the red pencil long ago, telling me I should begin at the beginning. And give you my name. 'Call me Ishmael' really isn't my style, but I'm Sherry, and my boyfriend's name is Mark. He's a teacher, too, Phys Ed by choice, though he does Sociology when the district needs the help. Mark and I have been together for three years now; have been talking lately about something permanent.

So, Sarah's imaginary pencil having been dealt with, on with the tale. Mark invited me to Montreal. We had both decided to take the summer off, him because he wanted to relax, me trying to write a textbook. I'm sure you can imagine how much progress I had made – the words kept getting in the way of what I wanted to say. So when he suggested some time in what he called 'real summer,' we fled Oklahoma for Canada without a qualm.

He woke me one morning with a suggestion. 'What do you say we get out of the city for a while?' He ran his fingers down my arm as he spoke, and my breath hitched in my chest. Mark has an athlete's hands, blunt-tipped and certain, beautiful to me. 'We could go somewhere we wouldn't need to be quiet.' He quirked an eyebrow, and I couldn't help but grin. On my agreement, he clapped his hands, delighted, and danced around the room like Snoopy to make me laugh.

He asked me if I'd do some shopping for him. I love to shop, for anything, may be the only person on this earth excited by groceries, so I took his lists and his money and bounced out the door, returning in the early evening, triumphant and giddy, waking him from his nap.

'You got everything, nothing missing, no problems at the stores?' Unlike me, Mark wakes quickly and all at one time, mind and body and voice all coordinated. If I didn't love him, I might almost hate him for that. His buzzcut means he doesn't get bed-head, either. But he sleeps nude, and for that sight, I'll forgive anything. I've often thought it a shame our culture prohibits nudity. He's better built than that statue *David*, and proportional even when he isn't aroused. I was too distracted by his body to answer his question, but he knows me. Rolling his eyes, he dragged the topsheet off the bed. Temptation briefly veiled, he repeated his question. I answered, and he rewarded me by dropping the sheet again.

We made love on the floor between the bed and the bathroom. You'd think there are better places, but it was more than fine – it happened to be where I was standing when the sheet dropped. After, he rushed me through a shower and out the door, our bags already packed, bill already paid. I hadn't realized he meant to leave that night, but what the hell? It was worth it to see him smile. And he did smile, excited and satisfied, all the hours he drove, at least until I fell asleep.

I woke sometime after dawn, still in the car. He leaned over me, planted a kiss. 'Good morning, sunshine.' I groaned, never at my best in the morning, but he just grinned. 'Coffee outside,' he offered, and I fumbled at the door. I didn't really look around until after the caffeine hit, but it was worth the effort to focus to my eyes.

It was glorious: Pines larger than I had ever imagined, hills rising all around us, no signs of people anywhere. Some birdsong in the distance, the sound of water. A dirt road, at the very end of which sat the SUV. A clearing, and a fire, presumably how he'd made coffee for me. He didn't drink it himself, said he already had two addictions, physical exercise and me. I loved that he'd make it, not bug me to give it up, though he did frequently suggest I could use more exercise. I usually told him that sex was my sport of choice, and dragged him to bed; it worked out well for both of us.

Sorry, where was I? Oh, yes, in the clearing on the first day. Mark told me there was no one near, and looking around, I could believe him. I took the chance to strip, baring my skin to the open air. Well, why not? Should I hide from the birds in the trees?

Mark came close, whispered in my ear. 'How does it feel?'

I closed my eyes to think about it. It was wonderful. The air caressed places it hadn't reached in ages, summer-scented breezes wafting over my skin. Outside, the air has textures you don't notice indoors all the time, and the sensitive areas of your skin feel them quite strongly. The more attention I paid, the greater the feeling grew, until I felt almost like the wind was my lover. I opened my eyes. 'Can we...? I mean, the ground might have bugs, or snakes.'

'We have blankets,' he laughed, 'and there's always standing up.' I'm sure my eyes lit. Standing is one of my favorite positions. I don't like to ask too often, because I'm sure it's a strain, but any time he's up for it, so am I.

'Care to give me a hand up, kind sir?'

He laughed.

Mark is a big man, six foot six, and built to scale. My head just barely reaches his collarbone. Height only matters when you're standing up, they say, but his length, too, is… um, impressive. My legs tight around his hips, my arms hugging his neck, my face buried in his shoulder, him the rod and me impaled on it. God, I love that feeling. It's like for once I can feel all of me. Words, words, always words. A container imposes its shape on the contained fluid, I tell the students in class, but in this moment, I feel like I am defined by what plunders me. I know where I am by his plunging, by his thrusts, and yearn ever closer to him as he reaches into me. We're monogamous, and I'm protected; there is no condom. He spurts and splashes and I quiver, spasming again. My climaxes press me around him, shifting, changing, ever and always myself, but different; known.

An absurd thought passes briefly through my mind: *Put two cats in Schrödinger's box and see what happens.* And then the panting and gasping and kissing and love-words, sounds whose meaning does not depend on language.

I almost complained when he told me we'd have to hike to the cabin, seeing it as a subversive attempt to make me exercise. But he offered to carry everything, so I shrugged and started to walk. I'm sure any observers would have thought it quite funny, me in socks and hiking boots and nothing else, him in socks and boots and backpack and tugging a sort of sled affair behind him, but as Mark had said, there was no one to see us pass. We rested often, drank a lot of water, stole the chance to kiss and fondle once we'd cooled, but still reached the cabin before nightfall. I thought I'd never seen a more beautiful sight, except for him.

There in another pine-bordered clearing stood a wood-framed building with giant clear-glass windows everywhere. There was nearly as much greenery inside as out, much of it with flowers, and a wide porch with a hanging couch for two. I sighed my pleasure, and Mark smiled. 'I'm glad you like it. Do you want the tour now, or would you rather have dinner first?'

My stomach answered for me, and he laughed and bowed me forward. 'What the lady desires, she shall have.'

After dinner, the hot tub, and tiny strawberries more flavorful than any I'd ever had. He used his hands and his mouth to bring me pleasure, half massage and half sex. I moved to return the favor, but he declined. 'I want to watch you,' he said, and, unaccountably, I blushed. I'd been naked all day, why was I feeling shy now? He asked, but as usual, I had no words to answer. He carried me to bed, drowsy with satisfaction, tucked me in beside him, told me to sleep well. 'Tomorrow is a day,' he said, and I nodded, owlish. It seemed the most profound thing I had ever heard.

I woke to what might be my favorite scents in the world: fresh-brewed coffee, clean aroused man, and oranges. It almost made waking worth the effort, and I blinked my eyes open just in time to see his smile. He turned away to place the tray on the bedside table, leaned in for an orange-flavored kiss. 'The rest of breakfast will wait until you're properly awake,' he told me, and levered himself up, striding purposefully away. When the coffee chased the cobwebs from my mind, I wondered where he'd been going, but food held more interest to me just then, and I forgot. The rest of the morning was just as lovely as the beginning, lots of attention to my tastes and pleasures, quiet moments alone. By lunch, though, I was beginning to have some suspicions. He held himself back a bit when we caressed. Stroked me, but never too far, too fast, too arousing. He seemed to be building up to something.

'All right, tell me.' He blinked, and I struggled to find what words would work. 'You're... planning. Working toward something.'

'Work?' He laughed. 'Darling Sherry, this is pleasure.'

For once I had words, and I leapt gratefully upon them. 'Work. As in energy expended toward an end.' Science is so concrete, even words have fixed meanings. Never so much as numbers, of course, but still. 'I can't see your end, but I know you have one.' I glared at him, and he tried his best to frown.

It didn't last long, though, and he fell down with the force of his laughing, then calmed himself with an effort and drew me close. 'All right, love, I'll tell you. First, you're right. And any time you'd like to see my end...' His eyebrows waggled. I said nothing, stiff in his arms, and he sighed and went on. 'This is going to be hard for me to explain. Maybe harder for you to talk about.'

'Did you know, before me, that you like your sex mixed with pain?' I bit my lip. It wasn't something I'd ever talked about before. He waited, and when it was obvious he wouldn't go on, I nodded my head in answer. Yes, I knew. I just didn't think about it, much.

'How far have you gone?' My head turned, my eyes met his, puzzled. I didn't understand what it was he meant. 'Oh, God,' he moaned, dropping his head on my shoulder. 'You haven't tried anything, have you? Never told a man you'd enjoy it if he hurt you a little. Never made a sound when he did to tell him to go on.' I made no reply. He knew, after all. I don't like words, don't trust them; how could I say to some man, 'hurt me, please?' How to convey the sense of limits, the particular kinds of pain I might like? And if I said it, there'd be no way to un-say it, later. You cannot 'eat' your own words once they've been heard.

'Right.' His breath hissed out in a sigh. 'Lady mine, Sherry, you do enjoy pain with your sex.' I slanted a look over my shoulder; he held up his hand. 'I'm just making sure we're on the same page.' I grimaced. Written words are even worse than spoken ones; they writhe on the page, changing their meaning each time you look. Not just from one viewer to the next, but between viewings! Facts aren't supposed to be malleable, but words alter the world. I made some primeval sound.

He massaged my neck. 'I know, Sherry, but sometimes words are what we have. Bear with me, will you? From what I've seen, you're not a masochist. But pain once you're already aroused seems to strike you as pleasure – please pardon the phrase – and I'd like very much to explore your limits there.'

His hands stroked my back, my shoulders. His breath parted my hair, his body supported mine. He was silent for as long as I needed, while I thought things over. 'You want to hurt me,' I ventured at last.

I could feel him shrug, his body shifting mine. 'Well, yes, if it will please you. I want to make you happy, whatever that takes.'

'Words!' I turned in his arms, straddling him, staring. 'Tell me.'

His body was hard beneath me. He pulled back my hair. Hands wide, cradling my skull, he bend my head back, biting the sweet spot below my jaw not quite tenderly. All my breath fled my body at the sensation, splinters of pleasure jagged throughout my form. I moaned when he stopped.

'You'll have a bruise if I keep that up.'

'There's no one here to see!' My voice was desperate, strident in my own ears. 'Please…'

'You'll have to let me know how far I should go.' He met my eyes for a long count, until I nodded. And then he reached for me with those long, strong hands. If I thought I knew him after three years together, that day showed me how much further I had to go. From the dazed look of awe in his eyes, it was a mutual discovery; he used his hands so roughly I thought I might die, and I begged and pleaded for him, not to stop, but to go on. At one point he had his entire hand within me, and though I literally could not breathe, still, I came. Oceans of pleasure washing out from within me, till I felt so light I could fly… More pleasure than I had ever imagined, he brought to me, until at last I slept.

I woke sated and sore and starving, met his worried eyes, and smiled up at him. He sighed, relieved. Carried me to the hot tub, hand-fed me dinner. Tended my every need till again I fell asleep.

I woke the next morning feeling like the world had changed.

We took things very slowly for the next few days, to soothe his worries. I was fine. Relaxed and ready for whatever he might want to try. I worked a little on my textbook, lay in the sun, got used to the feel of the grass beneath my bare skin. He… tormented me gently, if those words make any sense. Sought to find the least pain he could inflict that would still bring me the pleasure I craved. It was lovely, caring and sweet, but I wanted him to push things. And finally, after about a week, I told him so, marshaling words like convict soldiers likely to bolt if given the slightest chance. 'Mark. Love. You did what I wanted. And I loved it. I'd love for you to do it again. To hurt me.'

'Damn.' He paced, eight paces across, two to turn, eight again, repeated endlessly. A journey to nowhere, steps like letters across a page. 'We need new words.' I laughed, harsh caw with no amusement, and he stopped, one foot still raised, cocked a grin at me. 'You know what I mean. I don't really want to hurt you. I just want to do what brings you pleasure, even if that includes pain. God!' His own laughter sounded almost like crying. 'Can you imagine what Sarah would say about that line?'

We giggled together like schoolchildren, finally gasping to a halt. 'Teachers are supposed to communicate.' We both knew the phrase well. Tension eased, he looked soberly at me. 'Attend,' he suggested. I shrugged, waiting for explanation. 'It's a word some of the kink-groups use.

I think it came from English public schools. It means, kind of, give you what is needed. A servant attends a master, a student attends class, a nurse attends to a patient... a master attends to his servant's schooling...' I didn't understand why his voice had changed there, but it didn't seem to matter. He took a deep breath, shrugged, and went on: 'One attends to whatever is needed; whatever is needed is done. Attended to.'

I stared. Not at him, through him, lost in this bizarre thought. Why *not* use a word's malleability to my own ends? It felt rather like I'd been hit in the head with a hammer, but for the lack of pain. A word could be made to mean what I decreed. 'Attend.' I breathed it, savored the feel of it on my lips. 'Attend to.'

He nodded, solemn as a judge. Waiting.

I took a deep breath, stood, walked over to him, took his hand. Felt the strength in those long fingers, strong, joined to a palm almost larger than both of mine put together. I raised his hand to my lips, placed a kiss in that palm, folded his fingers over it, pressed down. 'Mark, love. I'd very much like you to attend to me.' The phrase felt right as I said it, so I said it again. And then, greatly daring for me, I told him what I dreamed of. 'I want to feel your hands... striking my ass.'

His eyes lit up like I'd sparked a fire in his soul, and his cock leapt about, drawing ciphers in the air. 'Are you sure?' he whispered the question; I could see him holding himself back, waiting for me to answer. I smiled, hugged him close. Nodded, my chin rubbing over his breastbone. 'I love you,' he told me, and lifted me in his arms.

He took me to the porch, to that lovely swinging couch, sat down on it, laid me over his knees. One hand rested on my back, the other delved between my thighs. I knew he could not see my face, but still I blushed. I was so excited; I'd dreamed of this for years. He chuckled, a warm sound that wrapped around my body, shifted my position, pushed off to make the couch swing. I gasped, I couldn't help it – I was afraid that we might fall. He just murmured something comforting, and waited for me to still.

I don't know how long we were there, just swinging, him petting me. It felt like hours, might have been, or only minutes, I can't say. I haven't the words for time passing in that fashion. It felt right, that much I do know. I felt kind of like I was floating, supported only by Mark, surrounded by his love for me. And then there came a sound that I felt through my body, a sharp crack like a tree falling in the woods.

Of course it makes a sound, I thought inanely. *The tree hears it; they've proved that plants respond to noise.* There was a pause as the sound shivered through me, faded away to warmth. Then again, a crack which shook my frame, redefining me. I sighed, feeling the breath warm as it crossed my lips, eddying with the cooler air around my face. A sudden sharp breeze above my ass heralded the next strike, and I closed my eyes to listen more intently.

Pain which isn't pain, but pleasure. Pain that sounds like music, heard with the body, not the ears. I couldn't tell if my senses were jumbled, or just my sense, but as his hand kept falling, I decided I didn't care. The words could mean whatever they cared to, I was busy, climbing toward pleasure, spurred by his hand on my ass. He tells me it was fifteen strikes, that first time, before I screamed and climaxed. I knew only that I was once again suspended in time, deep slow waves of glory lapping out from where his hand met my flesh, sinking into me and out again. His hands wrote patterns my body could understand, and I was grateful. Words? Who cared for words when I had this? I hoped he'd written them deep, that I'd wear them for a lifetime.

I told him so, later, and he laughed and shook his head. 'Nope, not even red anymore. I was gentle. It was your first time. But, if you're serious…' he cocked his head.

And that evening, as I curved over the stone he'd prepared for me, as I waited for the strike of the cane on my ass, my eyes poured over with love, and excitement, and my new understanding. My tears glinted in the light of the torches he'd set out, and I watched them fracture as they fell, delighting in their rainbow dance, imagining rainbows soon to bloom on my skin: love-words written by his attention to me.

Cat Fight at the Lucky Seven

Stan Strap

STANFORD STRAP leaned his forearms on the hitching rail outside the sheriff's office and smiled contentedly. It had been a quiet day in Smarts Ville and even the threatened trouble from the Mario brothers had come to nothing. Luckily for them they had decided at the last minute to go and have some fun terrorising locals elsewhere. Stan smiled again as he watched as the sun began to dip behind the mountains and the sky began to turn from deep pink to red. It was just the colour of Suzee Moon's bottom when he had spanked her last week. He thought too of what had happened afterwards, which caused him to straighten up and stamp his feet a little. It wouldn't do to let the minx dominate his thoughts. He did after all have a town to run. Perhaps a little tour of the streets before dark would be in order. And if his tour ended at The Lucky Seven then so much the better. He waited a few minutes while the shadows of twilight began to seep around the corners before moving slowly and nonchalantly into the darkening town.

At first, Stan was pleased to be able to report to himself that all was well. The good folks of Smarts Ville (6) were at home and safely locked in for the night and the remainder (173) were obviously at the saloon. The streets were utterly deserted.

He heard the noise from the Seven as he turned the corner in to Main Street and, on hearing the cheers, he thought for a moment that Miserable Pete was treating them to a few verses of *Spread A Little Happiness* but he quickly realised that these were not cheers of derision. The level of shouts, cheers and whoops meant only one thing: a fight. He quickened his step, tutting to himself and prepared to sort it out.

He paused for a moment at the swing doors. It was all very well making a dramatic entrance if the room was reasonably quiet to begin with but today with the place packed and the raucous crowd facing away from the door it would have been a waste of time.

He considered firing a single shot into the air but the last time he had done that the bullet had gone straight through the ceiling and nearly emasculated the mayor as he got ready for a session with one of the girls upstairs. He decided instead to go for the tap on the shoulder technique, which is what caused Big Dave to spin around with a glare. Seeing Stan, his glare turned to a cheesy grin and he tapped the person in front of him. Gradually, the room fell silent and the crowd parted as Stan stepped forward.

He didn't need to ask what was happening. Two of the girls were holding Miss Kitty by the arms and another two were holding back Suzee Moon while in between them crouched Nervy Derek, the bartender, praying that they were being held tightly.

Stan's eyes turned steely: a cat fight. This was not a simple matter to be resolved by the judicious application of fist to chin. He looked from one to the other of the combatants. The tousled hair and ripped bodices told the whole story.

'It was her,' Kitty began.

'No it was not. She started it by…'

Stan held up his hand. 'Both fighting, both to blame,' he said.

'That is hardly fair,' said Suzee.

'I'll tell you what is fair,' said Stan. 'You'll both take my belt across your backsides. Twelve each. Can't say fairer than that.'

Both women began to wriggle at once but the other girls tightened their grip. They were certainly going to enjoy seeing Miss Kitty taken down a peg or two. And as for Suzee Moon with her Kansas airs and graces, they were relishing the thought of hearing her squeal.

'But surely we can negotiate an alternative,' said Suzee as she and Miss Kitty were being bent over opposite sides of one of the large tables.

'There is an alternative,' said Stan as he organised things so that each woman had a girl facing her across the table pulling her by the wrists on to tiptoe and another at her side holding her by the waist to keep her bottom at the correct angle. 'The alternative is: no spanking, no job. You can leave now and pack your case. I won't have fighting in the saloon. Not under any circumstances. So what is it to be? Miss Kitty?

'Spanking,' she said through gritted teeth.

'Suzee Moon?'

There was a long pause and the room grew quieter.

'Spanking,' she said at last.

There was a murmur of approval from the crowd

which Stan silenced as he walked around the table, clearing onlookers to allow himself a full swing. When he had walked around a couple of times and satisfied himself that he had sufficient room he nodded to the girls and they raised Kitty and Suzee's skirts and petticoats to the waist in one swoop much to the delight of the crowd.

The two miscreants were almost facing one another and Stan wondered if Kitty was still glaring at Suzee as his first swipe with the broad belt landed full force across both cheeks. He moved slowly and purposefully around the table knowing that Suzee would hear and dread his footsteps as she waited her turn in the hushed room. She gasped in shock as he swung the belt hard against her upturned bum. Walking back he wondered who would be the first to call out. For call out they both surely would by the time he had finished. He could see Suzee watching him as he drew back his arm and let Kitty have it again across both cheeks.

After four each the women were trembling, clenching and trying to sway as soon as he stood behind them. He motioned to the girls to hold them tighter so that they should not escape even a fraction of the punishment he was going to dole out to their smarting bottoms.

It was on the seventh that Kitty threw back her head and yelled unashamedly as Stan switched to an upward swinging stoke that caught her just where her bottom met her thighs. Without Stan's assistants to hold her down she looked as if she would have leapt over the table. For a moment Stan thought he saw Suzee smile at her boss's discomfort. If so it was short-lived as he quickly moved around and did exactly the same to her, with the same devastating effect.

Stan waited until both women had stopped trying to hop from one foot to the other before switching to a diagonal roundhouse swing that sang through the air before landing on Kitty's tender behind. She threw her head back again, opened her mouth in shock but could not catch her breath enough to scream. Stan watched Suzee's eyes widen before moving around and laying a broad stripe across her. Both women lay shaking, bottoms clenched tightly.

'I sure am surprised at you ladies,' Stan said as he shook his head. 'I thought you would have known better, Miss Kitty and as for you Suzee Moon, I thought that you had learned a lesson last time. You will have to have some extra lessons or folks around here are going to think I'm losing my touch.' There was a ripple of laughter but as far as most folks were concerned they preferred not to think about Stan at all.

'You better listen up, all you girls. I won't have fighting in the saloon. Let's hope you all take telling from this,' he said. 'But just in case anyone is in any doubt, any repeat of this and it will be over the fence with you at the Fair next month and you'll take six from each of the lucky six winners of the raffle.'

'Put me down for ten tickets,' said Nervy Derek from the safety of his bar.

'And what's more,' said Stan ignoring him, 'you'll take it with your backside bared for all to see. Understood?'

Stan took the total silence as complete comprehension.

'And so,' he said very deliberately, 'the last four.'

For the next three strokes he moved swiftly from one woman to another in quick succession as they cursed then begged, then pleaded as he lashed their quivering bottoms. He paused for a long moment before the last. Both Kitty and Suzee had their eyes tightly shut and he dealt with Kitty before laying a vicious stripe right across the centre of Suzee's stinging bum.

'They must be blazing under those drawers,' Derek called out to general laughter. This time Stan did not ignore him. 'Good point,' he said. 'I will need to inspect the full extent of my handiwork to make sure the lesson has been learned.'

'It has! It has!' said Suzee and Kitty in chorus.

Stan sensed the bated breath in the room. He could see Nervy Derek and others licking their lips salaciously.

'But I shall carry out the inspection in private.'

There was the faintest murmur of disapproval.

'Unless anyone has a problem with that...' He looked around.

Everyone seemed to take a sudden interest in shoes and the ensuing silence was broken only by Suzee Moon: 'Well, yes I do as a matter of fact. I don't see why...'

'Will you be quiet,' hissed Kitty. 'Let's quit while we're ahead.'

'Upstairs, ladies, if you please.'

'And you call this being ahead,' Suzee whispered to Kitty as they shakily climbed the stairs ahead of Stan.

'Compared to the alternative, yes.'

Stan let them into the room that is always kept for him and then locked the door. He could hear the piano start up again and the laughter and raucous sounds began to grow as the tension eased downstairs.

He looked at the two young women. Miss Kitty was staring at the floor but he couldn't decide if Suzee was nervous as she looked around remembering her last visit;

or was there a trace of defiance as she caught his eye.

Dammit but she was a fine looking woman! But he had a job to do first and he was not about to shirk it.

'Right,' he said. 'Let me see if my lesson has been learned. Miss Kitty will take first turn. Kneel at the bed, if you please.'

'But, I'm in charge of the girls. I should watch Suzee take her punishment.'

'I want you to demonstrate so she will know exactly what to do.'

Stan's expression was implacable, so with a resigned shrug Kitty knelt at the bedside, hoisted her skirts to her waist and then laid herself on the bed stretching out her arms.

'Very good,' said Stan. He turned to Suzee. 'I hope you are paying attention.' He hardly needed to ask. Her wide eyes were a sure sign that she was both horrified and fascinated.

'Ordinarily', said Stan as his deft fingers undid Miss Kitty's drawers, 'just undoing this here string would be enough for me to know if the job was well done. But as punishment for a cat fight I want to see it all.' And with that he took hold of the white cotton waistband and pulled Kitty's drawers right down to her knees.

'Take a good look, Suzee Moon. Would you say that backside was completely red?' He could see for himself how the broad scarlet stripes from his stinging belt had criss-crossed her plump cheeks.

'Well?'

Suzee could only nod.

'I wish I could agree with you,' he said quietly before going over to the desk and sliding out a wide drawer.

'Oh no, Stan' said Kitty, 'not the switch!'

'Indeed it is,' he said extracting a strip of willow so supple that he could almost bend it into a circle. 'You will now show us how to take a switching bare.'

Kitty started to moan and complain but she made no attempt to move as Stan stood over her.

He raised his arm but he did not strike. Milking the hushed expectancy he suddenly said, 'the angle is all wrong. Suzee Moon will you take a couple of pillows there and place them under Miss Kitty's belly. Let's get that behind pointing up to me.' He smiled to himself as she asked Miss Kitty to lift up so she could place them correctly.

'Excellent,' he said before making a minor adjustment to her position before letting fly with a vicious downward swipe that made Kitty cry out immediately.

'Well done,' said Stan. He turned again to Suzee. 'That is how to receive the willow switch. No wriggling or leaping. You'll have noticed how the switch wrapped itself around her curves, and you can see the result.' He tapped lightly at a deep red line that had marked both cheeks, causing Miss Kitty to moan and clench tight.

'I see that your lesson is indeed learned,' he said. He watched Kitty relax with a sigh of relief and it was just at that moment that he let her have stripe number two, again right across both cheeks and no more than an inch from the first. It took much longer for her to stop shouting 'no' over and over this time but the second she did, Stan laid a third stripe between the first two. Kitty yelled then burst into tears.

He stood to make sure that Suzee was taking it all in before placing a firm hand in the small of Kitty's back then struck her five, fast, hard swipes as she buried her face in the quilt.

He stood aside again and watched Suzee's expression as she saw the full effect of the switching her boss had taken on the bare bottom.

After a few minutes Stan said, 'and now Suzee Moon, it is your turn. Miss Kitty, you may dress and leave the room.'

Kitty, tearful, pulled up her drawers gingerly and tied them loosely behind her before dropping her skirts. She stood up slowly and shakily.

'Did you say something, Miss Kitty?'

'It's not fair,' she muttered. 'She saw me but I don't get to see her take it.'

'Not this time,' said Stan, with reasons of his own for wanting to deliver the lesson in private. 'I hope you don't have a problem with that.'

'Definitely not,' said Kitty hastily, making for the door.

As she left, Stan caught the look of malice she glared at Suzee. 'I don't expect I've heard the last of this,' he thought. He smiled a Stan smile. Maybe next time they needed a lesson he would... or maybe... now that really would put the coyote in the hen house.

'And so Suzee Moon your time has come. You saw Miss Kitty; I want you to do exactly what she did. Correct position, please.'

Stan stood well back to admire the view as Suzee knelt, raised her skirts to her waist and then lay face down on the bed. He loved the way her full bottom pushed the white cotton tight. He could sense how tense she was as he slowly untied her drawers, and he too would have had to admit a certain tension as he lowered them to her thighs and saw her lovely behind still reddened from his earlier efforts.

'I feel sure that this final treatment will cure you of brawling in the bar once and for all.'

'I'm already cured,' said Suzee frantically.

'I doubt that. But in any case, I am a great believer in the phrase "better safe than sorry". And I am safe in the knowledge that you are going to be sorry. Sorrier than you realise even now.'

With that he brought the willow down smartly across the centre of her bum. A scarlet line appeared across her hot cheeks.

Suzee leapt up from the bed and clutched herself. 'No, no, no' she cried over and over. Stan waited until she stopped. She looked at him, caught his eye and then hoisted her skirts again before lying face down.

'You will remember how many Miss Kitty took?'

'Yes. Eight.'

'Good. And so shall you take eight.'

'Not another seven of those.'

'No. Another eight, for if you get up on your knees or move away at all... we start again. Start again, you understand me?'

Suzee nodded and muttered her assent. Stan watched her as she closed her eyes tightly. Still he waited as she tried to clench her buttocks as they quivered. While watching he carefully chose his spot. He noticed that just where the full curve of her bottom met her thighs there was a strip of pale skin that the belt had missed. He decided on a sideways stroke, a low arc rising up to bite into those soft cheeks.

There was a brief silence before Suzee let out a long cry: 'Aaaaaaaaah! Ouch, ouch, ouch!'

But she stayed down. Stan could see how she was trying frantically not to sway her hips away from him. He waited until she was perfectly still before repeating the action and catching her in exactly the same spot.

He nodded with satisfaction as she buried her face in the patchwork quilt and gripped handfuls of it. He saw her wriggle into the pillows as the heat from the switch rippled through her body. Stan could see the lesson was virtually learned but to ensure it he tried a third upward, curving shot twisting his body weight into the swing and catching her low again on her shaking bum.

Her muffled screams and shouts went on for a while and then suddenly she relaxed and seemed to be accepting the inevitable.

'Only four more,' Stan whispered almost tenderly.

Changing stance and rhythm, he placed three hard fast strokes right across the centre of her throbbing arse.

He listened as her sobs began to subside.

'After the last stroke I would be obliged if you remain where you are after your switching.' It was obvious that she was too far-gone to take in anything he said but never a man to shirk his duty, Stan raised the willow above his head and brought it down full force. As it wrapped itself around her curves Suzee lifted her face from the quilt and screamed through her tears.

Stan surveyed his work with some satisfaction. Suzee's bottom was bright red with a series of dark lines across her trembling cheeks. As he looked he began to take more notice of her smooth thighs, and the fullness of her blazing bum. He knew she was still not fully aware of what was happening but he could not resist kneeling behind her. As he did so, he undid his belt buckle.

Suzee tensed at the sound. 'Oh no, please, nothing else. I'm sure I'd faint under the belt now!'

Stan pushed his trousers down to his knees and moved closer to her. He revelled in her compliance as she raised each knee to allow him to remove her drawers completely. He was delighted to find her wet and slippery as he pressed insistently against her.

'It's time for you and me to ride into the sunset,' he said as he slid inside her.

Disobedience à la carte

Kit

'WHEN will you learn to be obedient?'
He sets down his coffee cup, wipes his lips with his napkin and grins at me across the table. I smile back, a fellow-conspirator. Obedience isn't the point and we both know it. I don't drive a hundred miles each way every weekend I can get away in order to be obedient; he doesn't keep his weekends free for me to obey him. Quite the opposite, in fact.

'You haven't managed well so far tonight, have you?' I can't stop looking at his eyes, eyes to dive into, to drown in. 'I asked for fish, you provided beef. Very nice, I might add, one of your best to date' - he's always polite, always complimentary – 'but definitely not fish.'

I'm always in charge of catering: he's a lousy cook. He washes up, and he's supposed to be in charge of menus: but, in fact, I cook what I want; the payoff's always worth it. After dinner on Friday night, we always sit for a while, listening to music; in the summer, we might go into the garden to watch the twilight thicken, to feel the night take on that rich, heady quality that goes so well with sex. Talking, digesting our week's news as our bodies digest our evening meal. I wait, in pleasurable anticipation, for him to signal that he's ready. It may be tonight; it might be tomorrow or Sunday. He watches me waiting, never misses a movement, a nuance. Sometimes he makes me wait so long that anticipation tips into impatience and I find I'm drumming my fingers on the arm of the chair or tapping my feet. He likes that, enjoys the power of it.

He doesn't demand much: it's not that kind of relationship. It's not lifestyle: that wouldn't be right for either of us, though we're both intrigued by those who do it, the psychology of it, the paradoxical security of extreme mutual dependence. We depend on each other too, but our lives have other priorities to be juggled.

He stands up and looks down at me, his six feet five to my five feet nothing; it's the signal I've been waiting for. Tonight we've been sitting in the garden and it's a warm, sultry night: we'll probably stay outside. I'm wearing what he asked me to wear in his email yesterday: a low-cut tee-shirt and a wraparound skirt. I'm wearing the high-heeled, peep-toe shoes he had made for me for my birthday; I've never had shoes so comfortable. No bra; just knickers. He clicks his fingers and I stand up, move towards him. He takes my wrists in his right hand – he has big hands: all the better to control you with, my dear – and raises my hands to his lips. He kisses my fingertips one at a time, slowly. My skin is prickling, my nipples throb; but I stand motionless. Not obedience, but anticipation: waiting for him to go on with what he's chosen to do.

He leads me down the garden, my heeling sinking a little in the gravel path. A short, taut washing-line runs high beside the path further down the garden, between two trees. He draws me close, reaches up to the line, pulls it downwards and gently entwines each of my wrists in a twist of it. That's all it takes. The other year, at a party, his friend Peter's wife asked him why the washing-line was so high and he told her, 'So I can make Veronica stretch,' and everyone laughed because they were a little pissed and thought he meant he enjoyed the sight of me stretching up to hang out the washing. I blushed a little, because I knew exactly what he meant: I couldn't reach the line to hang up clothes, of course, but I'd been there the night before, my arms stretched high above my head, straining on my toes to keep my balance, as he whipped me with another stretch of the nylon line. That left marks that didn't fade for over a week. When I went back the next weekend, he ran his finger over every mark very gently; but he used the nylon line again that weekend.

Tonight, he leaves me there for an hour, through the sudden, brief downpour that soaks my clothes and makes them cling to my skin. Before he goes, he slides his hands under my skirt, up my thighs and pulls my knickers up high, pulls the back of them into the crack of my buttocks, like a thong.

He says, 'You'll never learn to be obedient, will you?' and kisses me passionately.

Alone, I breathe the night in deeply, rain and all, waiting. I'm on two planes. On one level, the night, rain and all, is still warm, full of rich air and quiet. It's good, after the bustle of the city, just to breathe and be, to be made to accept some quiet time doing nothing else; nothing else but wait... On the other level, even though I know that for the space of a heartbeat now and then I'll wish he wasn't hurting me, the anticipation of the whip, the pain, the punishment is almost unbearable. My nipples press against the rain-wet tee-shirt, my pelvis moves in spasms against the cunt-wet knickers. They aren't comfortable and I'm stretched so high I can't really adjust them by wiggling; when I try, all I do is tighten the pressure somehow, until the material is rubbing hard between my buttocks, making my anus sore.

Raise a glass to pain, discomfort and the paradoxically liberating thrill of being bound awaiting punishment.

When he comes back, he's carrying something. He puts it down on the ground before he comes over and strokes my damp hair, kisses me, calls me his lover. I've never known anyone whose kisses are so horny. After a while, he gently pulls my tee-shirt out of my skirt and rolls it up slowly over my stomach and breasts, over my shoulders and my arms. He settles it comfortably across my eyes, carefully adjusting it to make sure it won't fall over my nose and mouth. Then he undoes the bow of my skirt and takes it off. I feel the washing-line move as he drops the skirt on it. He pulls my knickers up tighter, a little roughly, exposing maximum skin; when I cry out, he brushes his hand gently over my mouth to quiet me.

He moves in front of me and runs his hands over my face and neck. He cups my breasts, rolls the nipples between thumb and finger. It's all so slow and gentle, so horny, that my breath catches in my throat.

He says softly, 'Now, let's deal with dinner. I asked for fish with new potatoes and green beans, and you cooked beef and pasta, with salad. How many disobedience points is that?'

I go through the figures again in my head, although I already know the answer; I knew it when I planned the meal. There's a sliding scale; he's been adding to it for years. I calculate every stroke of my disobedience. It's a little like counting calories, though more dangerous, more of a gamble and far more fun: place, time, means and method are all up to him, and hand action isn't counted so I never know entirely what I'll get. Beyond the catering, I am never involved in planning for the weekend, and there may be other whippings; but disobedience *à la carte* is shared, a constant ritual.

I say steadily, 'Thirty, I think,' and he kisses me again and says, 'Thirty-five: red wine not white.'

He moves away from me. I hear a rustle of clothing as he bends down.

'Thirty-five, then,' he says.

'Yes,' I say.

He says, 'When will you learn to be obedient?' and gently smooths the whip he's chosen for tonight over my breasts. I recognise its caress: a stiff, leather strap, some four inches wide. Even though I'm expecting it, the first stroke of the cold leather, little more than a tap, makes me jump. I concentrate on the place where the leather landed: it feels wonderful, a promise of things to come. My legs go weak and adrenaline prickles through me in a hot wave.

He uses each of his whips differently: with this one, he never does more than five strokes on a breast without a break and there's a good pause between each stroke. Tonight, he works quickly, the strokes steadily increasing in force. The pain makes my blood pound in my ears, and I can feel pulses ticking frantically in my wrists and groin.

With the tee-shirt acting as blindfold, I'm focused on the sound, which is what he intends. The sounds of sadism are so horny: the silence before the stroke, the swish of expectation, the smack of contact, the silence settling again, these are at once terrifying and intoxicating: for him, too, he once told me during our early negotiations. 'I love the sounds you make when I punish you,' he said. 'When you breathe, when you whimper, sigh, cry out. Most of all,' he said, 'I love the way you want more, I love the way you wrap your arms around me when I'm through, I love the way you still love me.'

Five and five. He kisses me and runs his hands over my stinging breasts, feeling the heat he's raised, pinching the hardness of my nipples. He slaps each breast once, twice, then runs a hand over the skin, bends his face to mine and thrusts his tongue between my lips. He slides his hand lower, over my stomach, over my pubis, between my thighs. He pushes my legs apart and smacks my crotch, once, twice and a third time for luck. I gasp into his mouth.

He steps behind me. He strokes my neck and back with the strap, smoothing it downwards to my buttocks. There's a pause, then he seizes my hips and pulls me round slightly, positioning me so my back arches more and my bottom is pushed out towards him.

'How many more?' he asks.

'Twenty-five.'

He begins with five on my back; that's not his main area of interest, nor mine either, but it's a useful place to get rid of the odd numbers and to prepare me for what's to come. Then he settles in for the main course, slapping the strap across each buttock in turn again and again, harder and harder, the leather growing warmer and warmer. With his strap, he makes me focus, purges the worries and the irritations of the week out of me until nothing, *nothing* exists except pain and strap and skin, and the sounds of disobedience punished.

'Thirty-five,' he says at last. He drops the strap, holds me close against him and slides his hand through the slit of my skirt. Neatly negotiating the knickers, he thrusts two fingers firmly into my cunt. I gasp and twist against the restraint of the washing-line, trying to spread my legs wider, pushing against him as he works his fingers in and out, rubbing his thumb against my wetness and sliding it over my clitoris. After a while, I go a little dizzy, as I always do when I come standing up, and he swallows my cries in his mouth. He holds me gently through the sharp sweetness of my orgasm until I begin to breathe deeply again.

When I'm done, he unties my wrists, rubs them, kisses them. He picks me up and carries me to the house, to his room, to his bed. He takes off my shoes and my knickers. He massages me gently with lotion over my breasts and back and buttocks, pausing every so often to kiss my mouth or some patch of skin that appeals. Then we make love.

Tomorrow and Sunday, we'll continue the cycle of pain and pleasure, pleasure and pain. Alone on Monday night, I'll spend time with the mirror, being close to him: the marks on my skin help me bear the separation, I can see his love. By midweek, unless he uses a harder whip, the marks will have faded, leaving my skin a blank slate ready for Friday, ready for him to write a new chapter about disobedience and its consequences.

Next weekend is his birthday. I've worked out a real treat for him: grilled salmon with lemon and cream sauce.

He's asked for roast beef with all the trimmings. Roast beef, twenty; yorkshire pudding, roast potatoes and gravy, ten each; runner beans, five; horseradish sauce, five. Sixty points. If I change the dessert, I could bring it to seventy-five.

When will I learn to be obedient? Never while disobedience makes me feel like this.

And I'll spend the week wondering which whip he'll use.

Disobedience, Passion and the Unjust Whip

J.D. Jensen

'WHAT name have you, slave-girl?' the inquisitor asked casually. Yet the way he looked at her suggested that his interest lay not in her name, but rather in beholding her youthful beauty.

The girl was kneeling there before them. She had wide, innocent eyes that seemed to occupy much of her small pretty face.

There was a momentary hesitation, and then a timid voice replied.

'Aquistana.'

'Aquistana? Is this not a name which suggests obedience?'

The girl was at once confused. Instead of keeping her eyes demurely downcast, she looked up almost defiantly at her inquisitor. He sat in the centre of the panel, a grey-bearded old man on his left and a stern-faced woman on his right.

'Answer me, girl! Or is it that you know your own name is one that shames you?'

Aquistana opened her mouth to speak, but no words came. She only lowered her head, looking down at the mosaic tiles on the floor beneath her. The single robe that they had given her hung limply from her slender shoulders, scarcely covering the opening between the rises of her breasts.

The three panel members exchanged stern glances. Then the inquisitor said:

'You are sent here because you do not please your master. You are insolent and disobedient. How do you reply to that, Aquistana?'

'I… I… know not what to…'

She could not finish, her words coming hesitantly, and not as she wanted them to come.

'So, here then we finally have a slave who denies not the truth of her master's deposition.' The inquisitor gave a mocking little laugh, leaning forward on his seat, peering closer at her.

'A slave who admits her failings is perhaps halfway towards redemption. Yet, I see no contrition… neither in your face, nor in your demeanour. Although you kneel there before us, the haughty manner of your kneeling lacks servility or contrition. But are we perhaps mistaken with our judgement? That is, after all, what we are here for… to adjudicate between master and slave… before we decide a fitting punishment. Have you nothing to say for yourself, Aquistana?'

There was much she wanted to say, but she only murmured in a small voice, not understanding how her demeanour displeased the inquisitor. 'No, sir. Nothing… nothing that would matter.'

'Nothing that would matter?' he echoed. 'Then you admit your master's allegations?'

Again she could not answer, only giving a tiny little shake of her head. The inquisitor sighed, shrugging. He looked at his fellow panel members, then waved his hand curtly at the two guards standing behind the girl.

'Strip her.'

Immediately the guards came up close. One of them bent down, quickly grasping the loose folds around the neck of her garment. Then with a single powerful flourish he ripped it from her shoulders with such force that she lost her balance, needing to steady herself, her knees scrambling awkwardly to regain her posture.

There was silence in the chamber. The panel members only looked at her critically in her abject nakedness. Yet, all the same there was perhaps a measure of admiration in their eyes. Her frame was sleek and well-sculpted, the youthful covering of muscle and sinew smoothly rippling beneath her lightly-tanned skin. Her limbs were gracefully long and slender, and the twin peaks of her breasts were like firm little hillocks, proudly moulded and without the slightest droop in the pert angle of their repose. And her hair was like a goddess's... a shining mass that was swept back as if defiantly behind her dainty little ears, held in place by a cheap clasp of bone.

Once having regained her kneeling stance, she placed her hands as though protectively over her breasts. Her body seemed to clench itself inwards, as if to curl herself into a ball of modesty. She squeezed her legs together more, closing the crease between the little twinned rises of her pubis. Such crude disrobing had been shocking to her, and the humiliation made her face burn hotly. But she knew there was nothing she could do to entirely conceal her intimate places... not from the impure gaze of the onlookers.

'Ah! So, you have shame in your nakedness, yet no

shame in your disobedience?' the inquisitor challenged her sneeringly. But still the girl did not reply, her eyes downcast.

'Put your arms down by your sides and sit straight on your knees. Lift yourself so that we should see all of you.'

There was a hint of irritation in his tone, his eyes seeming to bore into her... and between the slender fingers that pathetically cupped the neat roundels of her orbs and her nipples.

Slowly the girl did as she was told, a slight tremor to her body. She raised herself, stretching her long neck out so that her angular jawbone was thrust forward almost proudly. Only then did she remove her hands from her breasts and put them by her sides, nevertheless daring herself to look up at the panel, feeling as if she were being defiled by their very scrutiny of her brazen nakedness.

For a moment there was silence. Then the inquisitor demanded:

'When did your master last whip you?'

So direct was the question that she could scarcely avoid answering it. For a moment it seemed as if she were thinking of when that last whipping must have been. Yet the inquisitor had observed no marks upon her anywhere. Her satin-like skin was unblemished, no faintly lingering telltale traces of lines upon her shoulders or buttocks.

Then, at last she answered in a clear crisp voice:

'My master does not whip me...'

Her words hung in the renewed silence. Then the inquisitor got up from his seat and strode over to where she knelt, slowly circling her, all the while his curious eyes examining her, perhaps looking for conflicting evidence, seeking out her lies.

Her back was so straight and erect now that he delighted at the way the small knuckles of her spine stood out so starkly. He marvelled at the trim narrowness of her waist, noting the way her hips swept out widely and curvaceously, each sphere resting so prettily on her feet.

'Then if he uses not a whip, he uses a cane on your rump?'

'He... he does not cane me.'

Clearly these were words he did not want to hear. He was standing right behind her now, looking down upon her. For a moment he pondered her answer. Then slyly, as if he might have discovered her half-lie, he ventured:

'Then he uses leather thongs on your rump! Or perhaps he flays you between your legs... just where the twinned rise of your coupling-entrance comes.'

She shook her head.

'Raise yourself onto your haunches and let me see.'

With that he placed the toe of his velvet slipper between the scarps of her buttocks and levered her upwards with his foot, lifting her, fascinated at how the lean muscles of her upper legs tensed and rippled at such irreverent movement.

'Open your legs out,' he instructed. 'No... remain kneeling there upright... knees spread. More!'

He bent lower, peering first under her bottom. Then he leant right over her shoulder, looking down between her breasts and in front to where the V crease of her open thighs was exposed for his inspection. But it was clear his curious eyes found no fading telltale residues of black welts anywhere. The inquisitor was confounded.

Never before had he examined any slaves that had been sent here without finding the welts and bruising of the aftermath of their masters' anger and frustration. Yet here, on this beautiful creature, there was not a single mark upon her flesh. Like some exotic bird her plumage was the very essence of perfection... just as if the gods themselves had created her.

Now, with a knowing little smile coming to the corners of his lips, he nodded, wisdom as if having given him the explanation. He said mockingly:

'Ah, no, Aquistana... your master is more discerning, I think. Not for him the crude use of whip or cane or thongs... or the marks they make upon his property. He enjoys punishing the inner perfection of your body.'

He bent over her again, his mouth close to her ear, speaking in an exaggerated whisper.

'He BOLTS you each time you show your disobedience! Is this not so, girl? Speak!'

She was confused again. What word was this? What punishment did he mean... that perhaps her master beat her with an iron bolt? She recoiled at the idea, denying it hotly.

'No, sir. He hits me not with an iron bolt. Not with anything.'

The inquisitor's eyes narrowed dangerously.

'What insolence do you talk now, girl? I said nothing of being beaten with iron!'

'I... I know not what you mean...'

But at that moment the inquisitor put his toe into the valley of her rump, and then pushed her viciously forward.

'Down! Insolent girl. Get down on your hands and knees.

More! Bend down low and thrust yourself back at me.'

Reeling with shock and humiliation she quickly arranged herself in this new debasing posture. So tense was every fibre of her body that it seemed her spine would arch until it broke, and so taut were her leg muscles as she tried to hold her thighs aloft in the way he had commanded.

Now squatting down behind her, a withering scowl upon his face, he placed one hand on each of her buttocks and prised them apart, exerting pressure to widen the gulf. Then he peered deep into the shaded cleft. It was the small round extremity of her velvety puckered sump that his eyes focused upon. For several seconds they dwelt there, seeking out the evidence he wanted to find. But there were no signs of any forced expansion of her passage, neither any soreness there, nor any such other indication of a recent bolting there. The girl trembled all the while, he feeling it through his fingers as they continued to hold her cheeks apart.

He peered in closer. Then another idea came to him and he released her.

'Bend lower. Spread your legs more.'

She could scarcely go lower, but desperately she tried to arch her body more acutely, making her rump push upwards towards him so as to accommodate his impure inspection. She was like a puppy-dog now, with its hindquarters up in the air, front paws on the ground. Her nipples icily touched the mosaic pattern of the cold floor, and the tremor to her legs was as if she had been seized by the ague of some deadly sickness.

Now the inquisitor squatted down behind her again. His face was so near to the taut cleft of her rump that she could feel his breath upon her skin. Yet, despite her anguish she resolutely kept her head raised up and angled forward, not even glancing backwards at him out of the corners of her eyes. She was conscious of how he peered deeply into her, such that it seemed as if the focus of his impure gaze would pierce beyond the very portals of her femininity.

What thing did he seek out in her private place and what 'bolt' did he mean? Ever since sunset, when she had been brought here, she had understood so little.

'It is a place where slaves are first assessed, and then schooled... for them to learn... so that they shall appreciate their masters all the better... if indeed the slaves should eventually return from there, wiser from their instruction and punishments,' Sollinicus, her master, had told her in that tone of his that suggested his exasperation with her.

He had continued then, almost sadly. 'If the gods only knew how much my heart and soul have been rent asunder by your sullen treatment of me, Aquistana, surely they would spare me the further torment of permitting your daily presence... never smiling, always cold... unwillingly obedient but only to show your disdain for me, as if you despise your poor master. And those big eyes of yours! Always so insolently they regard me!'

For some while she had nurtured the merest suspicion of it, but not really suspecting that his feelings for her were anything beyond what any master would have for a lowly house-slave. True, she was sullen, but only because of her deep inner sadness. After all, she had nothing to rejoice at, she so far from her home, from her family and her people. Loneliness and sadness were her only daily companions, together with her fading memories. She would go about her tasks mechanically, but not without sufficient diligence and care, and always obeying silently, bowing at his every command.

Only that one time had he beaten her, more out of his frustration at her silent acquiescence, than for any actual misdemeanour. She could recall the occasion vividly, but more with resignation now than anger. Certainly she had felt that initial fury and humiliation rise within her like a volcano at the time. Her eyes had smouldered with hatred for him at her hurt pride and demolished dignity, when eventually he had turned her and looked into her face.

'I shall beat you like I would beat a naughty child,' he had announced, beckoning her to where he was sitting. 'Lift your robe up! Higher. Now come over my lap.'

She had complied meekly, silently and with as much dignity as she could muster. Bending across his bared knees, she had immediately felt the icy tingling shock as her smooth belly touched his hairy skin. Lying there rigidly in that awkward poise, her bottom exposed in such naked abandon, for a few seconds it was as if he had become paralysed by the intimate burden on his legs. Then he had pushed the hem of her robe further up her back with a trembling hand, as if the target were not already sufficiently free of impediment. She had felt him shift his balance. Then she was aware of him raising his arm high above his shoulder, before finally the palm of his hand came down hard on her right buttock.

It was more the shocking unfamiliarity, rather than the actual pain that had made her yelp aloud, her pelvis jerking involuntarily upwards. Without a moment of delay the next stinging blow came on her same right buttock. But then, as if he had somehow recognised the need for a fairer distribution, the next blow had come to her left flank. For this he had needed to lean back slightly to accommodate the more confined sweep of his arm. Then the blows had come randomly, six or seven, she was not sure precisely how many, so humiliated had she been and seething in her silent fury.

She could recall, even now, how flushed his face had been, and how he was breathless at the end. She had glared back at him with smouldering eyes, yet saying nothing, until eventually he had pushed her away irritably, before getting shakily to his feet.

Thereafter he had scarcely raised his voice at her – perhaps ashamed at his own anger – even though she could tell his exasperation as he watched her going silently about her work, never so much as a trace of a contented smile upon her face, and now more sullen than ever before.

He would chide her. 'Your face is like the cold stone of idols, frozen in their perpetual frowns of disdain for living mortals.'

Then he would add, 'I command you to be joyous while you work, and when I look upon your countenance you will smile back at me. This I order you.'

But she would ignore him, hurrying to complete the task and gliding silently from the room. Then he would shout after her:

'Other masters beat their slaves for less. Whereas I never beat you. And I dress you in finely-threaded robes and not the coarse linen of ordinary slave-girls. And do I not put sandals on your feet so you do not walk bare-soled in the dusty ground? And I feed you not with servants' gruel, but with the same lean meat that you serve at my table... and still your eyes are black cold beads that avoid my gaze.'

All these recollections came to her, even as she knelt here in such debasing posture, conscious of the impure proximity of her inquisitor, and wondering still at his words. What thing was this 'bolting'? She had no concept of it, knowing only that whatever it was it could scarcely be desirable.

But now, as her mind deliberated in vain, he touched her between her legs – this time his fingertips alighting on the backward thrusting pouch of her femininity. The shock made her gasp, her body giving a little shudder of objection, even though she knew better than to pull away. Concentrating, she kept her body rigid, every nerve-end crying out; every muscle and tendon straining; the cold fury of her soul contained within. At first his finger only circled her satin enclave. Then she felt a fingertip trace slowly along the central slit of her puckered hood, nudging into the soft pulp between. It was as though he were exploring her, or perhaps testing the limits of her complicity.

But she did not deign to react, only holding herself yet more rigidly, even if the soft folds of her tissue had become as dry as desert-sand, the natural moisture of her inner private sanctum as though sucked out by the wicked invasion. Her upper legs were like the youthful trunks of willow trees, lean, lissom and strong, anchored determinedly to the ground beneath, and holding her body poised there with a natural gracefulness that defied the debasement of her posture.

She closed her eyes, willing his finger to withdraw. But it did not, instead only pushing further in, at once encountering the gossamer membrane of her resistance. She felt the tiny pulses of his excitement then, as the irreverent tip of his flesh felt around the drum-tight skin, curious for where the natural tiny breach would be, before then finally locating the narrow channel and wiggling itself into the confined perforation.

'Ahaha, girl! So you have denied your master his lustful entry into you? Or perhaps he denied you the privilege of his own entry into you?' The inquisitor seemed incredulous, even that his own lust was high. 'Furthermore I can see that he has put no bolt in you as punishment.'

The inquisitor was clearly perplexed, but he was still searching the soft intricate labyrinth, as if to finally confirm that he had not been deceived. Again Aquistana felt his grunting breath upon the spread valley of her rump.

'So, your master neither beats you, either with leather or whip, nor does he bolt you, by all accounts. He's indeed a most patient man... not even visiting his own bolt of flesh upon you.' The inquisitor sniffed at her, she hearing how his nostrils took in her sweating scent.

It was then that he withdrew reluctantly from inside her, his finger slipping out from her only slowly, letting the folds of her tissue close again gently over the impure void of his departure.

'Yet still he sends you here, all the same... for us to teach you respect for him and to make you obedient...' Here he paused, before adding slyly, '...and not least for us to administer the deserved punishment that he himself declines to give.'

The inquisitor sighed, rising to his feet and standing back now for a moment, studying her hindquarters. Then he glanced over at the two other panel members and without a word being exchanged between them, the man and woman only nodded.

He turned again to the girl below, seeing how she was still as rigid as some stone sculpture in that perverse bottom-thrusting poise. He marvelled at the illicit beauty. Perhaps he would even commission the Roman artist, Felitaveus, to fashion some erotic statue for him of a girl in this servile posture, he thought vaguely to himself, the sudden notion at once pleasing to his senses.

But the inquisitor became businesslike again, speaking down to the slave-girl.

'Obedience is best taught by showing the errant pupil the consequences of such disobedience... so the wake of her agony will linger enough to remind the pupil that obedience is preferable to disobedience!'

He turned then to the guard behind and curtly ordered:

'Bring me the black Learning whip.'

Aquistana heard the words, a tiny pulse of fear surging through her. But still she did not move, keeping herself no less rigid than before. Neither did she turn her head so much as a fraction, even when she heard the guard's heavy footsteps hastily returning. There was a brief silence, and then a muted rustling sound... and then finally an evil little zipping swish, as if some tensile shaft of leather had sliced the air.

A coldness crept into her heart, and a little shudder of unwilled anticipation seized her body, causing a momentary weakness in the taut muscles and sinews of her legs. Even though the whip had only swiped uselessly at the air – perhaps in a cunning act of torment designed to sharpen her fear – the sudden brutal movement was almost as if she had borne the full brunt of its delivery, her bottom having flinched with involuntary expectancy.

He laughed.

'Oh, yes my proud beauty. You may well quiver. Though, when the stinging blow eventually comes to your pretty mounts you will do more than quiver. You will suffer the pain of a dozen scorpion stings, Aquistana. Not just one lash but several, until I'm convinced that your lesson's learned... and that you will henceforth obey, rather than defy your master's wishes.'

Again there was silence from behind her. Without moving her downcast head, Aquistana glanced up beneath her eyelashes at where the two panel members still sat. Devoid of all emotion, they coldly watched her dejection. She could almost see from their eyes when the inquisitor's blow was going to come. But still it seemed he was in no hurry, the leather hovering there above her rump, tormenting her, waiting for the moment. So cruelly heightened was the tension, it came almost as a relief to her when finally the blow was unleashed... a vicious downward swipe that cut simultaneously across both crests of her rump.

'THWAAACK.' The sound of leather on flesh was starkly loud, seeming almost to echo around the stone expanse of the chamber.

She gasped out, a quick secondary breath catching in her throat. The impact made her jerk forward, her body seeming to follow the momentum of the strike. But even before she could recover herself from the shock she heard another faint zip against the air again, and once more the leather bit painfully into her twin crests, barely a finger's width below where the first delivery had drawn its evil livid welt across them.

'THWAAACK.'

This time a little cry escaped her lips, her body arching in a spasm of excruciation.

'Aaaagh... ooooph.'

She squeezed her eyes shut while the first wake of stinging agony made the nerve-ends of her tissue scream out in silent protest. Her hands had rushed back to clasp tightly at her buttocks, her fingers desperately seeking to smother the two throbbing welts.

But then, through the red haze of her agony came an unexpected sound. At first she wondered if it had come as a dream. Yet she knew the voice at once.

'Stop! Enough!'

It was Sollinicus, her master. And now suddenly he was by her side, his face etched in remorseful concern, and he was lifting her; kissing her; crying.

'Forgive me, my poor lovely Aquistana. Forgive me, I beg. Henceforth you are not my slave. Could you not see my love... and how it came so thick and fast upon my heart that it spilled out in wicked cruelty...?'

And then she was in his arms, her trembling nakedness against the warmth of his body, her tears running freely.

Broken Vows

Ruby Kola

MISS WILLIAMS clicked the top of her red Bic pen and threw it into her sturdy canvass bag. She gathered up the assorted test booklets and stacked them into a neat little pile, secured them with a big butterfly clip and sealed them in a large manila envelope. As she slowly walked down the deserted corridor, the echo of her sexy black pumps bounced off the shiny brick walls.

She let herself into the registrar's outer office and deposited the envelope into the secure box. *Everything has to be so secretive in these private schools*, she thought.

She picked up the day's mail, a few memos and a small pink message slip. 'Miss Williams,' the memo read, 'please come to my office after completing the final examinations.' The note was signed *Br. Anthony*.

Tawny Williams had been teaching American History at St. Matthew's academy for three years. She had considered moving to a school that offered her a more lucrative contract after her second year, but something, or someone, kept her tied here. That someone was Br. Anthony.

She tapped lightly on his office door.

'Enter,' commanded a low, deep voice.

She slowly pushed open the heavy oak door and entered the warm room. The setting sun flooded the richly decorated space with golden orange streaks across the wooden desk. Br. Anthony Serrano was reading through a thick file and stared at her intently. He ran his large hand through his thick, wavy black hair then loosened his tie.

'Miss Williams,' he began in a serious tone, motioning her to have a seat, 'I'm concerned that you're not quite adhering to certain policies here at St. Matthew's.'

'Oh, really?' She crossed her long, sexy legs and gently slid up her pleated wool skirt over her knee.

He walked behind her and meticulously placed his hands on the back of her leather chair. 'You see,' he added, sliding his hands across her shoulders, 'you have some very impressionable young men in your class. We feel that perhaps your skirts are a bit too short.'

'Is that so?' she asked softly, uncrossing her legs. She felt his warm breath near her face, then his lips, demanding and firm against her neck. She quietly gasped as he kissed her, hungrily and urgently, sliding his hands into her blouse, and then tearing it open with one sudden jerk. Small pearl buttons scattered onto the burgundy carpet. He squeezed her breasts and fingered her nipples, pulling and pinching them until they were swollen and ruby red.

He came around to the front of her chair and knelt down. He slowly spread open her legs and gently kissed both knees.

'Miss Williams, you know what the punishment is for breaking the rules here at St. Matthew's, yet you continue to defy both myself and the history department board. I think it's time I taught you a lesson you won't soon forget.'

He took her by the hand and escorted her over to the front of the immense wooden desk. 'Bend over,' he said sternly as he opened a secret drawer and removed long silk scarves and a wooden slat with a smooth leather covering on the end.

'No,' she stammered, 'not that. I thought it would just be the usual routine today. I've never seen that before!'

The usual routine had been a weekly occurrence at St. Matthew's. Br. Anthony would reprimand her for some imaginary infraction then watch as she teasingly removed her clothing and stretched out over his knee. He would play with and massage her smooth white ass, spreading her cheeks open wide, fingering her anus and clit until she moaned and quivered. Just before she came, he would stop, making her beg for him to touch her again, to put his fingers inside of her. Then he would slap her ass, gently at first, then harder and harder, driving her to the brink of pleasure and pain until he couldn't hold back any longer and they made love on the thick burgundy Berber.

'Miss Williams, you will do what you're told and bend over that desk now, or regret the consequences later. You have been forcing my hand to administer this punishment to you for some time.' He pushed her back down until she was lying across the top, her hands underneath her face. She wondered what would happen next, both fear and excitement churning inside her. The desk felt hard and slightly uncomfortable against her large breasts, and she wished she were against something softer. He came around the front of the desk and roughly grabbed one arm, stretching it out toward the corner. He tightly tied the scarf around her wrist and then fastened it to something hidden under the top of the desk, maybe some kind of hook or knob. Then he did the same thing to her other arm, forcing her to crane her neck uncomfortably, the warm sun flooding her face. He pulled a small velvety pillow off the couch and gently slid it under her neck so she could rest her chin and she felt relieved.

Perhaps he was only playing around with something new, she thought. As Dean of the History Department, he was allowed to have a power trip every now and then. His forceful, take-charge attitude was one of the things she admired about him.

He walked around the desk and suddenly, without warning, slapped her hard across the ass. A quick stinging pain coursed across her bottom, and she let out a small scream and quickly twisted her body to the side. Even through her wool skirt and silky panties, the sting from his bare hand made her wince. She wished she could rub her tender cheeks but her hands were completely secure. Instead, she tightly gripped the edge of the desk in the hope that the sensation would quickly subside.

'I thought as much,' Br. Anthony smiled. 'This type of reprimand is something new for you, isn't it?'

He returned to the secret drawer and removed more silk bindings. He knelt down behind her and slowly eased his warm hands down the back of her legs, sending erotic chills down her spine. He eased her legs apart and tightly tied her ankles to the feet of the desk. She could barely move.

'Miss Williams,' he announced, 'you are one of the few lay teachers we have here at St. Matthew's, and surprisingly, one of our most popular. There is a waiting list of students signed up for American History. Even the parents are delighted with your modern teaching techniques.'

'So why am I here in this position?' she asked.

'Silence!' he snapped, making her jump. 'I am still your superior!' She shamefully shut her mouth and squeezed her eyes tight, expecting another hard blow.

Instead, Br. Anthony continued his lecture. 'St. Matthew's has decided to extend your contract and offer you a generous raise. However, the other professors from the department, who support more traditional methods, are a bit *concerned*, shall we say? They have agreed to the new proposal on one condition.'

Tawny thought about the other history department professors, all five of them older than her, and committed to teaching with a smack to the ear just as easily as a crack of the spine of a history book. Br. Anthony was the youngest ever Dean of St. Matthew's and many of them resented him for it. She was sure they resented her as well. She could guess what their condition was going to be: a secret paddling the same way unruly students were punished behind closed doors. She caught her breath sharply.

Br. Anthony drew near, leaned over her back, and whispered in her ear, 'I knew you would agree to this, for me.' He kissed her neck and slid his hands down her outstretched body. He gathered up her skirt and teased her clit with his long fingers. She could feel her panties grow damp. She moaned slightly and arched her ass up toward him. 'Ooooh, I could fuck you right now, just like this,' he grunted, thrusting his body hard against hers.

He stepped back and called loudly, 'You may now enter!'

The sound of the large oak door swinging open made her stiffen and tense. She wondered who was there, and felt humiliated at being bent across the Dean's desk. She shut her eyes.

'Miss Williams,' Br. Anthony announced, 'you will now receive your punishment as determined by each of your fellow colleagues. Perhaps then you will learn to exhibit a more humble attitude in front of your superiors.'

She nervously wondered what would happen next. Br. Anthony approached her delicately and slid a soft round cushion under her stomach, raising her bottom into a beautiful and well-placed target. 'Are we ready to begin, gentlemen?' he asked, gently slapping the leather paddle against his hand.

'Br. Anthony,' she heard a gravelly voice inquire, 'shouldn't her petticoats be raised?' To her horror, she recognized Br. Frederick's voice, an ancient professor who taught ancient history. *He's in for a surprise if he thinks women still wear petticoats*, she smiled.

But her smile didn't last long as Br. Anthony returned to her side, lifting her skirt and trying to bunch it up against the pillow. 'I think it best we remove it altogether,' he added, unzipping the back and sliding it down over her mounted ass. He untied both ankles so he could remove the garment completely and gingerly placed it on the leather couch, careful not to wrinkle it. *How could this be any worse*, she thought, trying to hold back a tear.

'And the panties too,' Br. Frederick added sternly.

Br. Anthony returned and placed his hands over her ass for a fraction of a second, careful not to betray their secret affair to the other brothers. He slid her silky red lace panties down over her butt cheeks and tossed them onto the floor before securing her legs once more.

'Each brother has elected to bring his own method of punishment,' Br. Anthony remarked, 'and each will be awarded two strokes. That's one dozen all together, a rather light sentence for such a virgin backside. The degree to which they administer the lashes is entirely up to them.'

She tensed her body in anticipation as Br. Frederick approached her naked bottom. 'You should have been given this a long time ago, girl,' he muttered angrily, then poked her sharply with something long and smooth. It felt like a riding crop with a small leather patch on the end. She braced herself as she felt the end of the crop lightly rub against her ass in soft tapping circles. She stiffened her body, shut her eyes and gritted her teeth as she felt Br. Frederick's body heave upward and heard the soft whistle of the air. The crop came down against her left cheek in a stinging burn and pain spread across her bottom. She jerked her body upward but silently remained tied to the desk.

'Didn't that smart, missy?' Br. Frederick laughed as he poked at her reddening cheek again. She held back the tears of pain and shame, unsure of whether or not to answer him. 'Well, this one will then!' he shouted as the second lash cut across the same left cheek.

'Oh!' she screamed, wriggling her body, instinctively trying to rub and cover her burning backside. The pain made her quiver slightly in a sensation of stinging heat.

Her eyes filled with tears and she shut them again tightly, trying to force the pain from her mind.

'Br. Michael, you're next,' Br. Anthony directed, as the younger man with pale blue eyes and long, sandy, shaggy bangs hesitantly approached her from behind.

Not Br. Michael, she thought to herself as she pictured the quiet, young man and her discussing reading material and assignments together in the teacher's lounge. *How could he participate in doing this to me?*

Br. Michael borrowed Br. Frederick's crop and without a word gave two fast slaps across her right butt cheek in quick succession. The blows were gentle and easy, but still stung a bit as she clenched and unclenched her ass to help relieve the pain.

She heard laughter and mocking from the other brothers as they all told Br. Michael he needed a bit more practice before he administered any punishment to the students! *Only three more left*, she thought, sighing heavily. Hopefully they will all be as gentle as meek Br. Michael.

'Br. Terrence and his well-worn tawse,' announced Br. Anthony as the middle-aged European History professor took his mark. Br. Terrence placed his hand across her tender ass and patted it lightly. His hand felt warm and soothing as he squeezed both cheeks slowly, one at a time.

'You'll feel this one, Miss Williams,' Br. Terrence grunted as the wide tawse cracked across her bottom in a deafening sound.

'Aaah!' she screamed, not expecting such force. Burning tears rolled down her pretty face. Unrelenting pain coursed through both cheeks at once. She could feel the other professors' silent stares boring into her, watching her ass redden and her body quiver and spasm.

'Shall I give you one more?' Br. Terrence asked firmly, bending close to hear her sniveling cries.

'Oh, please no,' she begged, 'I don't think I can take another one like that.'

'You insolent bitch,' he said, 'you think you're so popular? You ask me for another stroke or I'll give it to you twice as hard.'

With effort, she cried, 'Oh, Br. Terrence! I... I... please, give me another stroke.' She screamed as the second blow blazed across her burning ass. She thought she would pass out, as her knees wobbled and she buried her face into the little pillow under her chin. If it weren't for the silk ties holding her in place, she knew she would collapse onto the floor.

She couldn't believe they were only half finished! How could she take any more? Who was next? She tried to control her sobs and stiffened her body in preparation for her next tormentor. It was Br. James, an effeminate, effete homosexual from some small village in Northern England. He approached her and she could sense that he was staring at the ripening red welts across her cheeks.

'Hand me that paddle,' he said. 'The one with all those little holes. The boys find this one particularly painful. This should be a nice little lesson for you, my dear.'

She didn't think she could bear any more as Br. James bounced the paddle against her bright red bottom. She held her breath as she heard a loud whistle and whack. The paddle slammed against her ass and she violently jerked her entire body upward, trying to yank her legs out of their restraints.

'Ohhh,' she loudly moaned, 'ooohhh, no,' as the pain shot across her sensitive left cheek. Hot tears rushed from her tightly shut eyes once more. She braced herself as the whistle came again, even harder and more forceful than the first stroke.

Muffling her cries into the damp velvet, she yearned to touch her deep red welts and rub them for relief. She wished Br. Anthony would touch her, comfort her, make her punishers end this torture. But she knew he had arranged this for her benefit, to allow her to keep her position at St. Matthew's. Now only one more brother was left, and when he was finished, Br. Anthony would give her two very gentle and quick strokes and then it would all be over. How could she face this group tomorrow morning?

She knew the last professor in line was Br. Nathan, newly arrived from the Congo. He towered over six feet tall, with dark black skin and a booming deep voice which intimidated even the toughest of young men in his senior African History class. She sensed his large body approach her, then felt his large hand cover almost her entire bottom, crimson and raised with wide patches. As he moved his hand across her ass, the end of his fingers lightly glided over the edge of her pussy and she let out a quiet, raspy moan.

Br. Nathan stopped and looked at her. 'In my country,' his voice resonated deeply, 'we can provide a different kind of punishment to women who do not know their place.' He slid his finger against her swollen pussy, massaging her in soft little circles. He teased her clit, making her moan quietly while the other brothers stepped a little closer.

'Ah, so I see you like this,' he laughed, thrusting his long fingers against her clit. 'Tell me how much you enjoy this!'

'Oh,' she panted, slightly trying to spread apart her legs. She was aroused but sore at the same time, wanting him to enter her, to finger her into a deep long orgasm. 'Oh, yes, yes,' she softly whispered, her back arcing gently as little spasms jerked through her body.

'Do you like this?' he asked again.

'Oh, yes, don't stop,' she whispered. She was on the very edge when he suddenly pulled away, leaving her wanting more.

'Thank you, Br. Nathan, professors,' said Br. Anthony. 'I shall administer Miss Williams' final two strokes in private, provided she can demonstrate to me that she only deserves two more. Thank you for your time.'

As the heavy oak door swung to a close, she could hear the muffled, delighted laughter from her traitorous colleagues from the other side.

Thank God, she thought, *it's finally over*.

As the door eased shut with a dull thud, Br. Anthony rushed to her side, grabbing her by the hair. 'So, you enjoyed that little display from Br. Nathan, did you?' he cried, pulling her head back sharply with one hand and unbuckling his belt with the other.

'No, no!' she cried, surprised by his ferocity, 'No, I only want you!'

'It didn't look like it from that little display,' he said, pushing her face hard against the pillow. He yanked off his thick leather belt with a snap and folded it in half. He whipped it down across her sore ass again and again in heated fury. Crack after crack cut through her already painful welts. Then finally it was over. He threw the belt across the room and released the tight hold he had on her.

Her entire body heaved as she cried into the pillow. She yanked wildly at her soft straps, trying to free herself. As the burning began to ease, her sobs grew softer. She wondered how he could stand there staring at her. As she turned her head to the side to look at him, she heard an odd sound. He was standing near her, rapidly stroking his throbbing cock.

He reached over and fingered her wet pussy once more and she moaned despite her anger at him. He leaned over and spread her pussy open wide and shoved his cock into her. Pleasure flooded over her and she knew she would come any moment. He thrust into her deeply and fiercely, grunting loudly until her moans rose to gasping little screams. He pushed deep inside her, holding her body firmly and letting out a low cry. She tightened her body in one long, deep orgasm like she had never experienced before, then spasmed and quivered underneath him. He kissed her back and gently slid out.

She couldn't speak until after she was completely untied, rubbing her ass and wrists tenderly. She quietly dressed and gathered up the pearl buttons on the carpet. Br. Anthony was sitting at his desk, scanning over the thick file once more.

'Miss Williams,' he said, pushing a legal paper across the desk toward her. 'This is your new contract.'

She smiled as she saw just how much her new salary was. She knew she would be returning to St. Matthew's for at least one more year.

The Mercy of Strange Men

Aimee Nichols

LYDIA is ready. Lydia has been ready for some time. She has lost track of how long it has been since the Master prepared her in the usual way – naked and face down, her knees bent under her, upper body stretched forward so as not to put too much weight on her thighs. Arms out in front of her and tied to the edge of the platform with long leather cords. Legs shackled in the same manner at the ankles. This is the way they have always done things; the stretching pressure in her muscles has become as common a feeling as standing up or walking around. She has learned how to relax, how to breathe and move her weight about in order to delay becoming stiff and sore from so long spent in one position. Even so, she seems to have been here longer than usual. She is not sure how much longer her body will hold out without the promise of relief.

Surely the show should be ready to start soon?

Time moves excruciatingly slowly without the benefit of sound or images for distraction. Lydia tries to clear her mind and be calm, as the Master always tells her to do, but it's not as easy as she would like it to be. In isolation such as this, displayed to no one in an empty room, her vulnerability is almost unbearable, but enticing at the same time. She imagines how she would appear to an onlooker who might happen upon the locked room by some twist of fate, unaware of what was inside or why, shocked at their discovery, but a shock mingled with arousal, perhaps. The blue and red hues of the overhead lights cast purple shadows over her body, highlighting curves and crevices. The position the Master has posed her in pushes her ass out provocatively and gives her spine the exaggerated curve of sexual mythology without her having to deliberately arch it. Her long rich red hair tumbles over her shoulders, obscuring her face from view. Her breasts are heavy and round, and their weight extends from her chest, creating a buxom and enticing silhouette. Her pale pink nipples are fully erect.

Already her body has started to respond to the promise of what the night will bring, the consequences of being displayed in such a manner. She smiles, secret and sly. The Master will be pleased when he comes back and finds her wet with no external provocation. She awaits his return, as her cunt grows wetter and her skin ever more sensitive to the air and atmosphere of the room. This is where she belongs.

After an eternity of waiting, when her body has calmed from its initial arousal response but her mind still flares, her lust-heightened senses detect the door opening and the outside breeze wafting in to assault her bare skin, which prickles into gooseflesh in response. She hears the quiet shuffling and low murmurs of the audience taking their seats, and imagines what they look like, and what their reactions are as they look at her, exposed and subservient and untouchable on stage, like an exotic creature in a glass case.

They will have come here to see her having heard of her through the whispered grapevine of gloat and conquest. The thrill of that fact never fades. The familiar buzz of it starts in Lydia's mind and moves through her body, coaxing her nipples and clitoris to erection again. Unconsciously she arches her back, pushing her ass higher in the air and her hairless sex towards the crowd. She can feel their presence, their numbers growing. She can feel their attention and readiness; the air is sharp with their sexual tension. She wonders how many feign disinterest, and how many are unable to tear their gaze away, staring without shame, confident they are at last in an environment where they will not be judged and found guilty for looking.

The Master assured her one night, stroking her hair after a show in one of his candid moments (brought about by a job well done), that the men were fascinated by her. She had a large repeat audience. Those who did not return were normally forced by circumstances to stay away; the Master had shown her a letter on a different occasion, from a regretful former patron who had accepted a job interstate, but who wanted to tell them how important a part of his life Lydia and the Master had been, and that they remained in his fantasies. She had been flattered that someone like her, who did not attract second glances on the street as she quietly went about her everyday life, should have such an effect on a person, on many people, outside of those everyday situations and bonds. It was flattering, she reflected, to become a part of someone's sexual mythology, to have their thoughts turn uncontrollably to you and the brief moment you were a part of their life. To not even have to know them well or acknowledge their existence for this to occur. To know that even after one night in someone's presence, you were a part of their life forever.

Lydia had agreed on this arrangement, so long ago now, because the Master had promised to bring her out of her sexual shell. He promised that their experiences together would provide the sexual release that she needed so badly. She had been sceptical at first, even as her cunt responded to the scenarios and ideas he described. How was this supposed to liberate her? How was being naked in a room full of strangers watching her become a sexual object going to do anything to realise her own fantasies? In the end, she could not deny how much the idea spoke to her and excited her, and how in thrall to the Master she already felt, and how that thrilled her. Refusal was an available choice but never a realistic option. From the first night, her willingness to obey and experiment had rewarded her. After that, she could not pretend there had ever been any other reason for agreeing than her own sexual satisfaction. The thrill was too great, the arousal too real.

The room continues to fill up, the murmuring of the voices growing deeper and louder. The presence and arousal of the men is almost a physical force now, and it seems there are a lot of them. Lydia strains to detect the Master's presence on the stage, to hear the deep timbre of his voice even if his words are imperceptible.

She cannot, and despite her arousal she tenses. Surely he wouldn't leave her alone at the mercy of strange men? He would not go that far, she thinks, a faint chill of doubt crystallising in the back of her mind. He would not overstep her boundaries completely, despite his talent for pushing them further and further from what they used to be, despite the fact that they are unrecognisable compared to the boundaries she thought were unmovable before she started coming to him. But would he completely disregard her limits?

As she frets and begins to feel over-exposed in her bonds, she fails to detect the closing of the door, signalling no more admittance for the night's entertainment. Her worries cease when she hears her Master addressing the audience in his deep tones. She listens to him explain the formalities and rules of the night, and thank them for their attendance, promising they will not be disappointed. She imagines the long-time attendees nodding impatiently, aware of what they must do to stay, waiting for their arousal to be sated, and the newcomers concentrating on taking in everything he says, lest they commit some faux pas that will see them ejected from what they already know will be a very memorable night. The dark bass of the Master's voice ricochets though her body, and her yearning begins anew. She does not know what he has in store for her, but she craves to find out. Her waiting and anxiety will not have been in vain.

He finishes his speech and comes to stand by her side, positioning himself, as always, near her right hip. He is out of her peripheral vision range, and turning her head is forbidden. She tries to content herself with the knowledge of his presence and noting how she can feel his immense sexual energy even from a distance.

It is time for the show to begin.

'And what,' he coos in a voice loud enough for the audience to hear, 'does my little slut wish to learn about tonight?'

Lydia recognises the familiar opening line, tenses in anticipation of the erotic menu to come. Her cunt clenches involuntarily. She wonders if the audience is tensing too, knowing the outline, but not the content, of what is to come.

'Perhaps we could teach you about water-play? Some nice naughty droplets running down your body from one of our gentleman guests? Perhaps some live lesbian action between two supposedly heterosexual women – or is that more of a men's fantasy, my little girl? A dirty one for us boys and our incorrigible ways? I'm sure *nice* girls like yourself would never deign to fantasise about something so base and so unattainable, so unrealistic and *common*, because everything you would think of wanting would be romantic and attainable and not even the slightest bit vulgar. That's because nice girls like you think you don't have to beg for anything, isn't that right?'

At this he pauses momentarily to lightly brush his fingers across her vulva, spreading the wetness he finds there, and without thinking she thrusts herself against his hand. In response, he moves it away, and wipes her juices on her ass cheek, disdain obvious in the forceful drag of his fingers.

'As you know, my dear, and as our esteemed audience are probably aware by now, I take great pleasure in stripping young ladies like yourself of your illusions about these matters. I must say, I've never had any complaints so far.'

Lydia hears murmuring from the crowd, sounds of amusement and agreement. She imagines the men nodding their heads at her Master's words, pleased to finally have someone voice the thoughts they're not meant to think, looking down on her, and she flushes with embarrassment.

'But I've gotten off track, haven't I, my repressed little darling? We were talking about your lesson for tonight, how you want to show your debauched desires to our esteemed guests and prove the existence of the slut heart that beats inside stuck-up nice middle-class girls like you.'

It is always the same. It is lies and performance, a mask of exaggerated disdain for the benefit of the audience, but he sees inside her head and dredges up her darkest shame and desires, proving her to share the desires she considers contemptuous and base in others. He makes her acknowledge what she's been taught she should not yearn for. He scorns her for her needs; every man here is riveted by the forbidden lust that rages through Lydia's body and mind. Images flash through her head and she lets out a moan and pushes her pelvis back toward her Master, unconsciously offering herself to him.

'What is this?'

She doesn't answer. She can't, she's not allowed, but she wouldn't anyway. She knows what happens when the Master starts asking her questions.

'Are you trying to control what happens to you?' He says it quietly, but there is a resonance in his voice that she knows will carry to even the men seated up the back of the room.

'I think Lydia, our little slut, is trying to tempt me. I think she wants to control what happens to her. And I do not think that is appropriate.'

There is murmuring from the men in the crowd.

'I don't think girls who think they can be tied up with their pussies showing in public and not have to give up control to the men who know better than they should be allowed to get away with such cheek. What do you think, gentlemen?'

More murmurs of assent, stronger now, in the tones of men trying desperately to keep their arousal to themselves.

'Very well then.'

Lydia hears him walk away, off the stage, and the heavy footfalls of his return. He comes to stand beside her, but for several moments he says or does nothing, and she wonders what is to come.

A sudden harsh swishing sound cuts the air, and the biting sting of a riding crop burns across her ass. She gasps in shock and pain, and her stomach clenches involuntarily. The sharp pain always comes as a shock at first, even when she is ready for it and doubly so when she is not. It takes her body some time to adjust before she begins to enjoy it. But tonight the Master is not interested in giving her time, quickly bringing down the crop again, an inch from where he landed it the first time. Lydia cries out in pain, and tears sting her eyes. The crop bites into her flesh again, and her cry turns into a low moan. The Master pauses, and strokes her sore, tender flesh, whispering softly so that only she can hear.

She relaxes against his touch, knowing that it is only a matter of time before he hits her with the crop again. Sure enough, he moves his hand away, and she breathes in, waiting for the inevitable pain.

Her body is ready this time, and the sting carries with it a faint echo of pleasure. The Master rubs her ass again, the warmth of his hand mingling with her heat, and she relaxes and begins to breathe normally. He knows how to play her; he continues alternating lashes of the crop with gentle strokes of his hand. She begins to relish the hiss of the crop as it cuts the air, and her body begins to reinterpret the pain of contact as pleasure. Soon she feels the heat of her ass move lower down to her cunt, as she and the Master both knew she would.

He puts his fingers against her vulva and rubs it gently in a circular motion. She can feel his fingers savouring her wetness. He pulls his hand away and takes a step back.

'The slut must sate herself,' he informs the room in general.

He steps forward into her view but does not face her. He crouches at her side, not looking at or speaking to her, and unties the cord that binds her left arm. He then straightens, turns and walks back down off the stage without acknowledging her. She feels a momentary flash of disappointment at his lack of attention, but arousal takes its place as she hungrily places her freed left hand between her legs and begins to stroke herself. She rubs her clit with two fingers, giving herself over to sensation.

She strokes harder and faster, growling in the back of her throat as her orgasm approaches. The audience is silent, awaiting her climax, feeling the sexual electricity that filters through the room and crackles off the surfaces. Their collective gaze is riveted to the source of this energy; the woman who kneels, bound by leather ropes to the raised platform in the middle of the room, and sweats from the hot stage lights and her own palpable desire. Lydia feels their desire, their arousal at both the situation and the close proximity of so many other people, almost as strongly as she feels the sensations caused by her fingers working on her clitoris. She rocks back onto her hand again, offering her backside to the audience, and slips a finger into her cunt. Then two. She takes the pressure off her clitoris for a moment, knowing that if she delays her own orgasm, she increases the sexual tension in the room as well as her own eventual climax. Her thoughts fly to her Master as she finger-fucks herself, and she wonders what he makes of her display. Is he watching her, his gaze on her glistening pink cunt, watching the fingers thrust into it and come out a little more slippery each time? Does he have his hand on his cock as he takes it all in? What does he have planned for her after this?

She removes her fingers and goes back to stroking her clit, bucking again at the sensations. She will let herself come this time. She will come hard and noisily, and her sexual release will fill the whole room and everyone will be able to see what a little whore she is. The thought of all her men sitting there, thinking about what a slut she is and maybe with their hands on their cocks because of it, sends her over the edge. She comes to orgasm with a howl, rubbing her clit furiously and rearing back against her hand. She continues to rub even after she is sensitive, lost in a post-orgasmic daze and no longer aware anymore of the crowd and their various stages of arousal. Nor does she notice her Master is at her side until he has roughly grabbed her hand and bound it again with the leather.

She realises what is happening and lowers her head submissively. Although still recovering from her exhibitionistic orgasm, she focuses her senses on trying to locate where he is now that he has moved back behind her, and tries to guess what his next action will be. She does not have to wonder long before she feels the sting of a slap on her right buttock, and gasps aloud, out of shock more than pain, although she can still feel the trail of the crop across her flesh. Before she has time to recover her composure, a second slap lands with a sting upon her left buttock. There is murmuring rising from the crowd; they are excited by the Master's actions, and by her response. She arches her back and leans in towards the direction his hands are coming from, and is rewarded for her impudence by several more slaps, coming in quick succession across her ass. Her gasps come steadily, and morph quickly into moans. Then without warning he stops. She pauses, dazed, and whimpers for more, beyond capability of speech. She wants desperately to turn her head to see what is happening, but knows she must not. There will be a punishment if she does so, and far from being a continuation of what she has experienced so far, she fears it will rather be the cessation of the Master's touch, the premature ending of the show. The pause, however, is temporary, and she guesses it is for show. His hands come at her from her side, striking her in such a way as to slap both ass cheeks. She pushes back against his hand once more and is rewarded with several more slaps. She feels her responses grow more theatrical, mindful even in her aroused state of the audience. She wants them to want her, although they will never touch her in the way the Master is doing now. That's part of the point, she thinks, and makes a show of trying to squirm away from his punishing hands. Lydia, for all she has become, remains a terrible actress: there is far less show than genuine desire in her responses.

The Master stops, and as the pause lengthens, Lydia despondently comes to realise that he has decreed that part of the show to be over. She holds her breath and waits for him to begin the next stage.

She feels him kneel down behind her, and leans back to offer him her ass. He responds by spreading her cheeks, and keeping them apart with one hand, he rubs lubricant on her asshole. The lube is cold and unexpected, and she jerks away involuntarily. He pulls her back towards him and she feels him place the head of his cock against the tight ring of muscle, and braces herself for the pleasurable pain that she knows will come with his thrusts. Her ass is still relatively virginal, and any penetration comes with a heady mix of searing pain and intense pleasure. She does not know if the pleasure stems from the pain itself or the taboo of anal sex, and she doesn't care.

He plunges into her and she screams as he embeds his cock in her with an air of propriety, his left hand wrapped around her thigh so she can't try to struggle away from him. He pauses for a moment for her to take in the sensation of his cock in her ass, stretching her out, then withdraws almost all the way, leaving only the head of his cock inside her. She relaxes for a moment – too soon, as he thrusts back into her again with the familiar sensation of pain and profound pleasure. She begins to wail, a steady keening rhythm, an ode to the pleasure of pain and the pain of pleasure, in sync with his thrusts as they become more measured, and gradually the tone of her shrieks alters from the low pitch of pain to the high pitch of pleasure. She gasps in between squeals and rocks back against him, relishing the new sensation of pain this brings with it, a deeper sensation that is not as sharp as the pain of the initial penetration. He takes this as his cue to bring a new element to their fucking, and as he thrusts into her, brings his palm down flat on her arse in a hard slap which echoes through the room and through her tender flesh. She manages to gasp out a guttural request for more. Each slap sends a jolt straight to her clit, the sensation of her stimulation mingling with the harsh sting of his spanking and the ache from his cock up her ass, so that she doesn't know where pleasure leaves off and pain starts. He begins to spank her in time with his thrusts, and she writhes below him, not knowing whether to bcg him to stop or insist that he never does.

'You love this, don't you, you little slut?' he enquires in a voice loud enough for their captivated audience to hear.

'Yes,' she murmurs softly.

'Louder. I want our guests to hear. I want you to tell the whole world what a slut you are.'

'*Yes*,' she moans, her voice husky and raw. '*Yes, I am a slut, and I love this. I don't want it to stop.*'

He spanks her harder for her confession and she squeals again, her cheeks stinging profusely. She rocks back into him, and can feel the telltale throbbing that means his orgasm is building. He repositions his left hand so that he still controls her movements with it, but is able to stroke her clitoris with his fingers. She rubs herself against his hand frantically, then lets out a deep growl and comes again. The contractions ripple through her ass and set off his orgasm. He comes deep inside her with a grunt, and she feels his cock throb as it releases the hot streams of semen into her. She lets out a final moan and collapses under him, and his cock slides out of her well-lubricated and very well-fucked ass; her bonds, which had been stretched taut throughout their sex, loosen now as their prisoner sprawls on the floor offering no resistance.

She lies and pants, satisfied and looking up at him now as she is allowed to do once their act is over. He relaxes into a crouch to stroke her hair and looks back at her appraisingly, proud of what she has achieved tonight.

Behind them, the audience bursts into a raucous round of applause.

Lessons

Alicia Wag

CINDY showed up at his office around 6:15pm, dusk in April, the cruel month, or the new month, depending on whether you like poetry or flowers. She couldn't prevent these idle thoughts from running through her mind as she tapped lightly on the dark mahogany door, rapping her nervous knuckles on the smooth, warm wood, right next to the brass plate with his name on it.

'Come in.' She heard his voice, quiet but powerful. Just like his lectures, which she had been listening to for weeks now, trying to concentrate on them, ignore the uncooperative parts of her that led her to think about other things. Flights of fancy, you might call them, if you were looking for a euphemism. But Cindy didn't need a euphemism anymore. She could just call them fantasies now, and she was tired of pretending.

The door creaked softly as she stepped into his office and closed it behind her, turning the brass switch that locked it. He spoke first. 'Hello, Cindy,' he said.

He was sitting at his computer, the glow from it like moonlight on his face. As he waited for her answer, he reached for the lamp by his desk. Cindy put up a hand. 'No,' she said. He stopped, looked at her with a raised eyebrow. Surprised? Interested? Angry? The thought of him being mad at her sent shivers down her spine. 'I just wanted to thank you, and tell you how much I enjoy your class,' she said, trying not to stammer.

He leaned back, his mature, wise face smiling slightly. One hand ran through his impressive and dignified head of white hair, the other removed the eyeglasses resting on the bridge of his nose. 'Wonderful,' he said. 'Thank you.' He folded his hands and rested them over the bottom of his necktie, on his paunch. His fingers stroked the skin near his watch. He kept smiling at her in a disdainful, amused sort of way. 'Is that all?'

Cindy shifted her weight and felt sweat moisten the inside of her bare thighs. She had been at university for two years now. She wasn't a child anymore, not even a teenager, but she still favored a disciplinarian, and she had seen it in him from the first time she glimpsed him on campus. After two lectures, she had taken to wearing no underclothes to his classes. She thought about her body now, naked under her cotton dress, and a spasm of shame whipped through her. Still, she answered him. 'No,' she said, feeling the hot flush in her cheeks, turning her eyes downward.

His tongue rolled along his top lip, just touching the ends of his moustache. He swivelled his chair so it was no longer facing his desk. He gestured to the empty space before it. 'Come here,' he said with a hard slap on his thigh, an audible punctuation mark that echoed in the quiet dignity of his office.

The command made Cindy's nipples harden. She walked to the place she was told to go, like a good girl. 'Yes, teacher,' she said, biting her lower lip.

'Kneel,' he said, softer now, his voice a low hiss laced with a taunt. Cindy felt tears well up behind her eyes. She fought the urge to cry and beg him not to hurt her. Instead, she did as she was told and kneeled down. He stroked her yellow hair with his left hand, undid the buckle of his suit pants with the other. 'This is what you want, isn't it?' Cindy murmured assent, soft unintelligible sounds rolling from her lips. 'Isn't it?' he said louder, squeezing a clump of hair in his hands.

'Yes,' she answered. 'Yes, teacher.'

Keeping a strong hold on her hair, he said, 'Take out teacher's cock.' Cindy yelped now, she couldn't help herself. The cry escaped from her mouth like a bad, bad thing. She knew she would be punished for it. Quickly, she unzipped his suit pants and found the hole in his under drawers. The size of his cock made her gasp with pleasure. Oh, how she wanted to suck it.

Her mouth watered as profusely as her pussy as she whispered without looking at him. 'Please, teacher.'

He laughed, a harsh guffaw. 'Sluts like you need to suck cock, isn't that right?'

Cindy nodded, keeping her eyes down. He placed both hands on her head, rubbing circles on her scalp, scratching hard, grabbing, pushing her into his rod, which grew harder the closer she got. She let her whole face feel it, her cheek and nose and eyelids rubbing against the skin of his shaft and balls and hair. She buried her nose in the spot at the base of his cock, drinking the damp smell of his balls, the hair tickling her nostrils.

She began to lick and taste, her tongue lapping the clammy, soft skin of his balls. His dick was rock hard now, smooth and dusty pink, the red knob at the end shining. Cindy rolled the tip of her tongue around the gleaming head, tasting the sticky drops of pre-cum there. His hands forced her head down, pushing his cock into her mouth. She opened wide, letting it all the way in, letting it gag her.

She sucked hard and hungrily, her lips hugging tightly around him, taking him in and out of her mouth, feeling his cock press into the back of her throat. She had been wanting this for weeks, staring guiltily at his pants while he lectured and wrote equations on the blackboard. She had seen him around campus before even enrolling in his class, and she had to admit that this – his cock in her mouth and the price she would pay for it – was her only motive. Now she had it, and she wanted to lick it and suck it until it exploded inside her. She wanted to open wider and wider until she swallowed him, until he burst in her mouth.

But he stopped her, pulling her up by the hair until she was looking him in the face. 'Look at you,' he said, touching around her mouth with his fingertips. 'You have teacher's cock all over your face.' Cindy tried to go back down on him, but he held her hair hard. 'You are a bad, bad girl.' Cindy suddenly remembered her body, naked under her dress, and the shame returned in a hot rush through her body.

'Please,' she whispered. He grabbed one of her tits and rubbed it. The nipple hardened in his hand and he pinched until Cindy felt her cunt tingle. 'Please,' she said. 'I'll do a good job.'

He laughed again. Humiliation bloomed like a flower in her heart. She opened to it, knowing that her teacher would do what needed to be done.

He stood up, his erect cock still hanging out of his pants. 'I'm afraid you're a very bad girl, Cindy,' he said. Then he commanded, with that authoritarian slap on the thigh, 'Hands and knees.'

Cindy turned her body around until it faced the other way, leaned over, and placed her hands on the nubby carpet. He walked around and around, looking at her, stopping in front of her, coming just close enough so she stared into the head of his cock. The nearness of it filled her with that hopeless, pitiful longing again. Though she knew it was futile, she leaned forward to take him in her mouth – she wanted to suck him so badly. He pulled away, laughing at her. 'Please,' she said, her head hanging.

'That's no way to punish a slut like you,' he said. He began walking around her again, then she felt his hands pull her dress up to her waist, revealing her bare ass. He laughed out loud. 'See how naughty you are.' His hands caressed her cheeks. She felt how soft they were under his fingers, like the petals of the tulips that bloomed and opened outside her dorm. She began to moan.

One hand smacked her. She felt hot, unbearable shame overtake her and she let it go now, sobbing. 'Please don't hurt me,' she cried, even as she felt herself lifting her ass higher.

When his hand met her cheeks again, first one, then the other, she could feel every inch of his fingers leaving their mark, branding her. The skin of her ass stung and tingled. He grabbed it and squeezed, spanking her again and again, picking up the tempo until his palm fluttered hard on her rear, numbing it, making it alive. She lifted her hips higher, opening her legs wider every time his hand connected with the tender, hot skin of her bum. She imagined how he was marking her, the red welts his palmprint made, and she cried out to him, tears streaming down her face, 'Teach me my lesson.' She lifted her rear end higher still, moving up and down like she was fucking, exposing her wet cunt.

He spanked her stinging butt cheeks with one last burst, a long series of smacks, one immediately following the other. She imagined the movements of his hand, so quick they blurred, like the fluttering of a bird's wings. Then he stopped, caressing the sore skin and squeezing it hard. Cindy bit her lip until she thought it would bleed, suppressing the yelp of pain that gave her so much pleasure. She had already overstepped today. She hoped he would give her another chance. 'You can get up now,' he said. She stood, and lightly brushed her fingers against the skin of her numb, aching bum.

He sat at his desk, dignified and authoritative. Cindy saw that his cock had been put away. She felt a rush of desire, her mouth watering, followed by a hollow sense of desperation. 'Come back tomorrow at the same time,' he said, smiling in the darkness.

'Yes, teacher,' she said, and left.

The next day it rained, incessantly and heavily. Cindy skipped all her classes except his. As she entered the auditorium for his lecture, closing up her black umbrella and shaking the raindrops from her yellow coat, she caught his eye.

He peered at her over his glasses, resting serenely on the bridge of his nose, a small smile on his face with the slightest hint of a sneer. Cindy looked at his hand, a piece of chalk rolling between his thick fingers, and nearly swooned.

She didn't even bother to use her umbrella when she left the classroom, avoiding his eyes, and hurried across campus back to her dorm. Rain poured down her head, slipping off her coat and into her galoshes, soaking her to the skin. The cold wet drops found their way to the insides of her thighs, her warm pussy, all bare under her dress.

By the time she closed the door of her room behind her, she was sopping with rain and desire. She leaned against the door for a moment, panting with exhaustion and excitement, remembering what it felt like to have his cock in her mouth. She knew she had been bad yesterday, but someday he would reward her again. Someday, he might even fuck her.

Her thoughts and the anticipation of her meeting with teacher later in the day kept her from being able to accomplish any schoolwork. She spent the afternoon sprawled on her bed, sucking her black dildo and pretending it was teacher's cock, slapping and rubbing it all over her face. It was the biggest dildo she could find, and when she shoved it inside her the pain made her wince. She fucked herself hard with it until she came several times.

The rain subsided as Cindy prepared for her afternoon meeting. She put on her most demure yellow dress, a one piece cotton pullover with a turtleneck and a flared skirt. When she tapped lightly on his door, her skin was fresh and powdery dry, although the sound of his voice saying 'Come!' like a deep, dark bark made her sex moisten.

She entered, closing and locking the door behind her,

standing still, waiting for instructions. He was sitting in his leather chair again, at his desk. He'd taken his tie off, and left the top buttons of his dress shirt undone. A shock of white hair emerged from the opening and Cindy felt a thrill as she thought of his age, his power. He was holding something in his hands. It looked like a ball, though it was too dark to say for sure. He looked at it as he spoke, whatever it was, passing it from one hand to the next lazily. 'You were a very bad girl yesterday.' Cindy stayed quiet, trying to be better. He looked at her. 'Very good,' he said. 'You're learning.' He stood up and approached her. 'This will help.'

As he got closer, Cindy saw that it was a ball – a ball with leather straps attached to it, meant to wrap around her naughty little head. Her eyes opened wide with a mixture of disappointment and excitement. Ball gags made her drool and sometimes, if she moved enough, even retch a little. Of course she would rather have his cock in her mouth, but at least this meant he intended to punish her adequately. 'You made entirely too much noise yesterday,' he said, pulling on her dress. 'Take this off, and let's see what you have underneath today.'

Cindy slipped out of her flats and lifted the dress over her head, dropping it on the floor beside her. She stood before him naked and shivering with fear. He laughed at her, pinching her erect nipples. 'Slut,' he said. 'I'll have to take care of you properly.' He spoke with such tender menace in his voice that Cindy let a moan escape from her lips, she couldn't help it. He grabbed her still sore buttock hard and squeezed until she yelped. 'There you go again, you little noisemaker.' He lifted the ball gag to her face. 'Open your mouth.'

She spread her lips as wide as she could. He shoved the black ball into her mouth and attached it around her head. Already she could feel her saliva collecting around it. Teacher pulled at her nipples and said, 'I have just the thing for horny little nipples like these.' He pulled a clamp from each pocket and gently attached them. 'That's not too bad is it?' he asked. Cindy shook her head and he squeezed the clamps until sharp pain shot into her breasts. The ache was excruciating but she willed herself not to move or utter a sound. 'Very good,' he whispered. 'Excellent.' He removed the clamps and massaged each sore breast and nipple with his powerful hands. As Cindy watched them caress her, she thought of the complete mastery in them, how wisely they dealt her punishment and reward, and she felt her cunt swell.

He let her breasts go and said, 'Come with me.' Together they walked across his office and stopped in front of the red velvet couch in one corner. Cindy felt tears of terror well up in her eyes when she saw the whip lying on it, looking like a giant black snake. 'Now, now,' teacher said gently. 'It's for your own good.'

Cindy nodded, tears streaming down her face, over the ball gag, dripping down her neck and tickling her. Her jaw was aching from being open for so long, her nipples stung, and her sore pussy watered, but nothing could compare with the heat that was travelling into her buttocks, anticipating the crack of the whip. 'Get on your knees and hold onto the couch with your hands.' Cindy did as she was told. She felt the skin of her bare ass completely exposed and burning. Her whole body felt tingling and electric as she submitted completely to the will and care of her beloved teacher. As he lifted the whip from its place on the couch with one hand, she saw his big, swollen cock in the other, and she thought she could come just from the sight of it.

She felt a split second of cool breeze, then the whip landed on her creamy cheek. She winced and felt herself gag on the ball, then the whip came down again, lashing her skin, sending adrenaline keening through her whole being. She turned back and saw him pumping his cock with his left hand, his right hand fisted around the whip handle, his arm raised with unequivocal strength, coming down to mete out the punishment she deserved. The whip lashed her in rhythm with his hand wanking his cock, and Cindy lifted her ass each time to meet it, her ass numb and tingling, her heart melting with gratitude, her pussy hot with juice.

He spanked her so good, making her his girl, his slave, his prisoner. They moved together – his hand on his sex, the whip on her bum, her hips rising to meet it – until white liquid exploded from his dick, landing on the sweet welts with which he had marked her. He put the whip aside and she relaxed, rubbing his sperm into her wounds like healing lotion. 'Stand,' he said, breathing hard.

He unbuckled the ball gag and she spit it onto the floor, opening and closing her stiff jaw. He cradled her face in his hands, caressing it gently. 'You were very good today, Cindy.' His cock was still out, a stiff rod protruding from his suit pants. Together they looked down at it. 'Would you like a reward?' he asked.

Cindy nodded, a small nod. He put his cock away. 'Perhaps when you come back tomorrow,' he whispered, handing her the yellow dress and cradling the whip handle in his palm. 'Perhaps.'

'Yes, teacher,' Cindy said, slipping the dress over her head, 'I'll come back, tomorrow.'

Beloved Birch

James Baron

MICHAEL remained proud that he must be one of the favoured few still alive in England who had 'suffered' judicial corporal punishment – 'suffered' probably not being the right word since he'd discovered early in life that he was a hard-core sexual masochist for whom a severely-administered whipping was the ultimate in erotic pleasure.

In 1949, when he was just short of eighteen, he'd deliberately committed an offence which he hoped fervently would result in a merciless birching.

He had discovered his addiction at boarding school where, after lights out, they'd play games, the loser having to take a bare-bottomed thrashing with the buckle end of a leather belt. Michael found the pain produced a warm glow of sex throughout his body. Forced to masturbate in front of them following the whipping, he'd spurt in seconds. At home after his last term, a growing sense of frustration gripped him as his whipping and flogging fantasies mounted relentlessly. He'd no idea how he could turn them into fact. An encyclopaedia had informed him he was a sexual masochist. A history book he had brought from school – by accident? – contained a woodcut of a public flogging in the early eighteenth century. The victim, strapped to a post on a raised platform, was naked from the waist down and being whipped with knotted lashes by a burly fellow, also half naked. A large crowd flocking around the platform was clearly enjoying the spectacle. He would also clatter away on a portable typewriter, shaping excessive fantasies until he could write no longer and had to indulge in extended bouts of savage masturbation.

They say that the Devil has a way with the willing. One Thursday morning, Michael picked up the local rag from the mat and a headline sprang at him like a blow between the eyes. YOUTH, 18, GETS THE BIRCH! Michael raced upstairs into his room, and shut the door. Sinking on to the bed, his hands trembling, he spread the paper out.

A youth of eighteen had been given six strokes for stealing apples from a barrow. On passing sentence, the Magistrate told the Court that he intended to stamp on youth delinquency without mercy and that future youths facing him in the dock would do so at their peril.

Michael's fevered imagination raced into overdrive. The birch! Of course! He'd been thrashed with a belt, and caned – even tried self-flagellation with a dog-leash – but actually to have a birching would put his written fantasies to shame. It would be on his bare bottom, of course, and he could already feel the delicious sting.

There'd be people watching! He read the story again and again, noticing that the youth's name had not been mentioned. Well, that was something. The story said the birching had been carried out in the local police station. Hmm… well, he couldn't walk in and ask for a flogging!

This guy had stolen apples and got six strokes, but that wouldn't be enough! But what could he do to achieve his aim? Nothing big like trying to rob a bank, of course. Something more than stealing apples, though. He paced restlessly to the window and, as the sun glinted on the panes of the small green-house at the end of the garden, it dawned on him.

He'd throw a brick through a window in the High Street and not make a run for it! There was always a copper not far off. He'd wait until one got close and then – crash! Eighteen strokes, say – eighteen mercilessly hard strokes delivered by the strong, stern, impersonal arm of the Law.

But the pleasure wouldn't stem only from the whipping – there would be the undressing, the positioning: all the rituals, he imagined, which took place before the first stroke was delivered – and there would be others there to witness his pain and humiliation.

He mustn't, he mused, appear to be relishing the whipping too much – during it, he'd pretend to beg for it to stop, pleading for mercy.

He'd made up my mind: he'd do it on Monday and to hell with the consequences. This was Friday – and from now he'd mortify himself by abstaining from any sexual activity. That way, he'd be fully-loaded for the punishment, his bottom white, the eager flesh strained and ready for the delicious, biting sting of the birch. He would tell his mother nothing. She need never know. Anyway, since his father had left without word, she spent most of the time with a circle of friends from the riding club.

By Monday he was strung to the limit, his aching balls and cock pleading for relief. He bathed very thoroughly, put on a tight pair of underpants and, in a white shirt, school tie and grey suit, made his way furtively to the green-house, finding a half-brick, wrapping it in a sheet of old newspaper and stuffing it under his coat.

Luckily his mother was in her bedroom. 'Mama,' he called, trying to keep his voice casual, 'I'm just going into town to the library, won't be long.'

The High Street was busy with pedestrians and shoppers even though it was only just after nine. He selected a window – Rollason's the jewellers, with a huge stretch of plate glass – which he couldn't miss if he tried. He quashed any doubts in his mind as he paced back and forth. He wanted this more than anything: this need, this thirsting desire to be severely punished.

After five or six restless minutes a copper plodded round the corner towards him. When the man was ten yards away, Michael hurled the brick. Glass shattered. Amid the screams of pedestrians and the strident clanging of an alarm bell, the bobby was at him in a trice, grabbing his arm and dragging him away, swearing as he did so. Michael would have crawled, grovelled if he'd had his way.

In the charge room, a sergeant behind a high desk looked up 'What's this, Bill?'

'This is what this is,' Bill said, pushing Michael forward. 'Caught it heavin' a brick through Rollason's window. Glass all over.'

The sergeant stared down at Michael, tapping a pencil on his palm. 'Is this true?'

'No,' Michael said sullenly, 'It was an accident. This idiot…'

'Careful, son,' the sergeant warned, 'If you don't get

a birching for this, I'll eat my helmet.'

'The birch!' Michael thrilled at the words, but managed to utter scornfully: 'Huh – the birch, so what?' But his heart fluttered and his cock was struggling to escape. He gave his name, address, and age. Then his spirits sank as he was asked: 'Your mother and father at home?'

Michael caught his breath – what was this? 'Er, my father's gone, years ago.'

'Your mother?'

Michael hesitated. 'She's… out.' This was something he hadn't reckoned on.

'But she's there, normal, like? She'll have to be told.'

'But…' Michael began, feeling sick.

'No buts,' the sergeant said. 'Right, we can settle this soon enough.' He tapped his pencil on the desk. 'The court's sitting. You'll be taken there right after your statement.' It was short, and Michael signed it shakily, pleading guilty.

The sergeant leaned forward. 'I hope you get a damned good thrashing if the beak decides on it – and he will, mark my words! I just hope your mother's got the sense to give her permission. It's needed – you're under twenty-one, worse luck.'

Michael's throat was parched. His brain wouldn't function, but surprisingly he heard himself saying: 'My mother – what's she got to do with it?'

'I just told you, cloth ears!'

What happened next had a dream-like quality. His mother arrived looking pale – she'd been picked up in a police car. She avoided his eyes and he said nothing. In the courtroom there was a sea of blurred faces. He was told to stand behind a table – not in the dock – his mother just behind him.

The charge was read, Bill gave his evidence and the Magistrate stared at Michael grimly. When he learned Michael's mother was present, she was told to stand. 'Madam,' the Magistrate said, 'I'm now going to sentence your son. I shall ask you if you are prepared to sign a form agreeing to the punishment I shall pronounce.'

He stared at Michael again, intoning his full name: 'You have been found guilty of the sort of mindless vandalism which this Court will not tolerate. I intend to make an example of you. The sentence of the Court is that you receive eighteen strokes of the birch, which will be administered with your parent's permission, tomorrow afternoon in the police station adjacent to this courtroom at precisely 2:30pm.'

Michael's excitement at this left him faint with relief.

The Magistrate addressed his mother again: 'Madam, I strongly advise you to permit this punishment to be exacted – the pain and the humiliation may teach him a lesson he'll take note of. I wish every house had a cane or a birch in the corner and save the tax-payer the cost of the police doing the job for them. The Court is adjourned!'

Was she going to sign? The question drummed in Michael's head as he followed her out. She looked at him and spoke for the first time, her eyes glittering in anger. 'I don't know why you did what you did, but I'm going to sign the form.'

Michael's penis jerked.

'Well?' she demanded, 'Haven't you anything to say to me?'

Michael shrugged, trying to restrain his excitement. 'I... I...'

'That's enough.' She walked into the glass cubicle whilst Michael stood in the doorway. The words hammered in his head: *You're going to be birched. Tomorrow. At 2:30pm. Eighteen strokes.* His buttocks quivered. He heard his mother's firm voice. 'Where do I sign?'

A male voice: 'As your son is under twenty-one, Madam, you have the right to be present when the punishment is carried out. Do you wish that?'

His mother nodded. 'Yes, I wish to be present. Where and when?'

The sergeant wrote on a card and handed it over. 'The police station just across the way. Give this to the desk sergeant. Get there about a quarter-hour before so a doctor can check your son is fit enough for what he's going to get.'

'Thank you.' Putting the card away, Michael's mother brushed past him and he followed her out, his temples pounding.

Michael struggled to maintain his decision not to arouse himself. His mother was tight-lipped. He had little supper, and curled up in bed, kept his hands well away from his cock.

Not much was said next morning at breakfast, either. He ate cornflakes, crunched some toast and drank milk. His mother looked tired and strained. At one point he asked her briefly: 'What are you going to wear?'

'Black,' she replied curtly, 'What else? Get these

things cleared up, then tidy your room.'

Finally it was time to go. After his bath, he'd put on another pair of tight underpants – dark-blue this time – and the same shirt, tie and suit he'd worn the day before. At the police station, his mother handed the card over. 'Someone'll take you down,' the officer said gruffly, pressing an intercom button. 'The two-thirty party's here.' He flicked the switch and there was a thin-lipped grin on his face as he nodded at Michael. 'Sit down, son, might be the last time for a spell.'

After two or three more minutes of agony for Michael, a uniformed sergeant emerged, glancing at a clipboard. 'Come with me.'

Down a flight of stone steps, in a white-tiled corridor, a door was pushed open.

'In there.'

Michael, whose feelings were now so tangled that he couldn't make sense of them except for the word 'birching' ringing in his head, saw a small and largely bare room apart from a couple of chairs and a plain deal table. High on the wall was a barred window. A row of coat-hooks lined one wall of bare brick. Surely it wasn't going to be done here?

A second door on a far wall opened and two men came in. One, whom Michael would forever-after think of as *Waxed Moustaches*, had a red face and, under the glory of his upper lip, a full, ripe-looking mouth. He wore dark-blue uniform trousers, toe-shined boots, a blue shirt open at the neck, sleeves rolled to the elbows. Muscled forearms were layered with black hair. Michael knew instinctively this was the man who would whip him.

Thickness rose strong in his throat.

The other man was dressed in a dark suit and carried a black bag. His thin face was lined, his eyes sad and with bags under them.

Michael confirmed his full name and his mother, in a quiet but controlled voice, her status.

Waxed Moustaches read the charge from a sheet. 'You have been sentenced to eighteen strokes of the birch and that sentence will now be carried out.'

Michael cleared his throat. 'In here?'

'No, next door. Now, get undressed, and be quick about it.' He turned about and disappeared.

The doctor, for that's what he was, opened his bag. Michael asked: 'Do I have to strip completely?' He could scarcely get the words out.

'I'm afraid so,' the doctor said, bringing out a stethoscope.

'Is that really necessary?' His mother's voice was none too steady.

'Those are the rules, Madam,' the doctor confirmed, a sad note in his voice.

Michael, scarcely able to believe his wildest hopes were all coming true, crouched to untie his laces, slipping his black shoes and blue socks off. After he'd removed his jacket, his fingers fumbled so hopelessly with his tie that his mother helped. He got his trousers down and off and now there were just his bulging darkblue underpants. Rapidly he eased the waist over his glistening cock, let them drop, and kicked them aside. Naked and unashamed, shaking with fevered anticipation he stood there, staring at the wall.

After the doctor had checked him over without apparently noticing the strutting cock, he said quietly: 'I don't agree with this, but I follow the rules, I'm afraid. Look, son, it won't take long but it's going to hurt you a lot. I shall test you after each six strokes and if I feel you can't take any more then I shall order the punishment to stop.' He glanced at Michael's mother. 'Madam, are you sure you wish to view this? You can wait in here…'

'No!' Her voice was sharp. 'If what's going to happen to my son is partly my fault, then I should be there to suffer along with him mentally.'

The far door swung open. *Waxed Moustaches* stood there in a flood of white light.

The doctor nodded at him, and *Waxed Moustaches* crooked a finger at Michael. 'Come on, you.'

Stumbling, his cock bobbing, Michael knew he had reached his Mecca at last. There were others in the square room which he entered, but his gaze was focused on the structure which dominated it beneath a cluster of bare light-bulbs. It was shaped like a giant easel, a towering A. Halfway down the front of the A, a wide, leather-topped bench was set at right angles. From each edge dangled thick leather straps, two on each side, and at the base of the A, a solid metal bar joined each leg from which more straps hung loosely.

Michael heard a chair scrape across the stone floor, and glanced round. His mother was seated a few yards back, a uniformed constable standing beside her. Ahead of Michael stood *Waxed Moustaches*, a birch gripped firmly in his right hand. Michael's gaze was riveted on the instrument. The thick bunch of raw twigs was some three feet in length, drawn together in a stout wooden handle. Beside the frame stood a bucket containing three more birches soaking in water.

'Right, get over here.' As Michael shuffled slowly forward – already, he noticed, a thin thread of pre-ejaculation semen hanging from his stretched foreskin – others came into focus standing to one side, another sergeant, an inspector, a man in plain-clothes, and the doctor.

Before he was forced face down onto the bench, Michael gave a quick glance over his shoulder. His mother was sitting motionless, her black-clad legs crossed.

The leather was cold on his naked flesh, his penis painfully but ecstatically crushed into the surface. Straps buckled his wrists tightly, others bound his waist, and still more secured his ankles. He was helpless; beautifully, nakedly helpless. His buttocks, raised slightly by the tight belt around his middle, were poised, quivering for the first stroke. He could turn his head slightly to the side and the watching faces were set, intent. He had his audience!

A voice behind him: 'You know what your punishment is... eighteen strokes as ordered by the bench. I shall wait fifteen seconds between strokes. Are you ready to take your punishment?'

'Yes,' Michael gasped, his throat thick. He felt as if he might come even before the whipping began. 'Come on, please do it!' He heard boots scraping behind him. He squeezed his eyes shut. A swish in the air and the birch struck the centre of his buttocks with a slashing whip-like crack. An exquisite lance of pain seared across his behind and he shuddered with pleasure.

The fifteen seconds seemed an eternity, then the second stroke whistled down with expert accuracy just below the first. The third stroke seemed harder and below the first two.

Now his bottom was becoming alive with fire and the familiar glow was spreading over his body. He knew he couldn't hold his spunk much longer. How many to go? Another cut into him – the fourth?

The fifteen seconds between each blow appeared to be shrinking.

'Come on, number five! Harder... harder.' The fifth did seem more powerfully struck, and at last he could hold out no longer. Crushed to the leather, the eruption from the head of his twisted cock flooded hotly, soaking his upper thighs, muscles jerking spasmodically, the itch through the stem exquisite, and the birch cruelly lashed across him again and he let out a low moan of animal pleasure.

Then the sixth struck, searing the tender area below the curve of his bottom. He could smell his own semen and his sweat. The doctor was close, feeling his pulse, checking the artery in his neck.

'I'm... all right,' he panted, longing for the flogging to continue. Even though he'd come, he still thirsted for more. *Waxed Moustaches* appeared to his right, picked up a white cloth and wiped the twigs up and down. Some were broken, others bent. Bright red blood appeared on the cloth.

He was bleeding – and there were twelve more to go! The bent and broken birch was flung into the bucket and a fresh one brought out and wiped.

The boots shuffled again, getting a firmer grip he supposed. The flogging recommenced, fiercer now, the sharp bark of the twigs on Michael's tortured, swelling bottom accompanied grunts of effort from the flogger.

The doctor again – so that was twelve, only another six, worse luck. The thirst for more, many more, was unbearable. Michael gripped the wooden legs to which his wrists were bound, and prayed. 'Please! Harder!'

His buttocks screamed with pain as the lashing continued, and mentally he screamed with joy. His penis was growing again as the last stroke whistled into the spreading welter of unbelievable, unimaginable pain and pleasure. It was over.

Waxed Moustaches, breathing hard, wiping the beads of sweat from his forehead with the stained cloth, dropped the second ragged-twigged birch into the bucket. The room was still, so still that Michael could hear the clink-clink as the straps were unbuckled.

'Get up. I hope that's taught you a lesson you won't forget.'

Licking his dry lips, Michael managed to say hoarsely 'Uh, I won't forget it but not in the way you mean. You're a good whipper, you should do it more often.'

When Michael pulled himself stiffly to his feet, his bottom felt twice its normal size, throbbing, pulsating, dancing with erotic waves of fire. His punisher gave a long look at Michael's cock – it wasn't fully up, but nearly – and thin spunk still dripped from the tip: a pool gleamed on the black leather of the flogging bench. 'Most of them piss before it's finished, even do a crap sometimes – but I never seen anyone shoot their load before.'

The doctor was by Michael's side. 'Go back in the other room and I'll do something about your bottom.'

As he began to move, Michael heard *Waxed Moustaches* saying to the watching group: 'Didn't you see his cock when he came in here? For Christ's sake it was hard as a rock before I even got going. And look at that spunk all over the place.'

Inside the little room – how long ago it seemed – ointment and plasters were applied to the scarred swell of his behind. 'Your bottom will take some time to recover, some of the cuts are quite deep. Sometimes there's delayed shock after a whipping like this.'

Michael began to dress, pulling his pants up tightly. Emotions whirled: joy that he'd been flogged, disappointment that it was over, not disappointed though at the result. He could admire those welts and lacerations for weeks, masturbating and reliving the delight.

The Key to the Unknown

Sarah Dean

LEO examined his motives for one last time while he observed her through his open bedroom door. She was kneeling in front of the plate glass window, the evening lights flickering on her golden skin, her nudity invisible to the multitudes far below. She fidgeted with an auburn curl that had escaped from behind the blindfold. In the year that he'd known her, she had exceeded all his expectations. But he had to be certain that her obedience was beyond question, and for that she must pass his final test – however arduous. He closed his suitcase before he joined her in the drawing room of his penthouse apartment.

Beth reclasped her hands over her bare bottom and craned her neck while he sealed the three cream envelopes.

'Come here.' Her body rippled like a wild cat as she crawled across the pristine marble, seeking him out by his sound and smell, and knelt up to nuzzle lithely against him. She stayed still while he fitted the stainless steel chastity belt that she wore whenever they went out in public. She didn't flinch when the hinge sprang open and he snapped down the metal shield and drew the two thin chains up over her buttocks to hold it in position.

He checked that the lips of her labia protruded through the narrow slot that allowed liquid to pass but prevented penetration. The flexible steel traced the contours of her pubic mound perfectly, invisible under her clothing to all but him.

'There's been a change of plan. I'm leaving tonight,' he stated bluntly as he used the silver key to secure the padlock.' She sprang to her feet, smiling broadly. 'You won't be joining me,' he added.

It gave him some satisfaction that she betrayed herself so readily but still her unbidden tears touched his heart.

They dined by the river. The owner gave them a discreet table – the talented artist and the millionaire industrialist had already caused speculation. Leo ordered and offered no explanation for his change of plan and she didn't question him. Her courage in letting consequences take their course singled her out from other women he'd known. He'd recognised the same boldness in her work the first time he visited her warehouse studio behind Kings Cross Station.

They drove away from the restaurant and turned north, in silence.

'How long will you be gone?' she asked as evenly as she could when he stopped the car but an overhead train drowned his muttered response and she was disinclined to repeat her question – or ask him for the key.

'Get out,' he said flatly and rammed the powerful car into gear. He screeched away, leaving her on the pavement, the sobs tearing at her chest.

It would be two days before the first cream envelope dropped through her letterbox.

This afternoon you will compete in a tennis match. You must seek out and provoke the holder of the key. The metal belt will be removed while you find the full meaning of SURRENDER. When you have learned the lesson, it will be replaced and you must write to me.

I read your letter several times, trying to understand your motives. I have become so used to you that my banishment is like an open wound. Have I not given myself to you unconditionally? But to know you have parted with the only key is my worst pain. Your map was precise and the club was small and exclusive – but you know that. I wore the white pleated skirt that you like.

The match was mixed doubles. The other woman was a leggy blonde and the men, tall and athletic. Any one of them could have held the key. My partner was a skilful player – and a perfect gentleman. I have never worn the belt for so long and it chaffed my skin as I bent provocatively to retrieve stray balls, letting my skirt flick up, giving them all a perfect view of my knickers. But none of them could be diverted. We won the match but I returned to the locker room, dispirited by my failure to find the keyholder.

I was drying myself when there was a rap on the door. At first, I didn't recognise the man who had umpired the match when he stepped into the room uninvited.

'Just locking up,' he excused himself but his eyes ogled me as I clutched the towel. 'Not so shy on court, were you, miss?' He came closer and I flushed with embarrassment, reminded of my flirtatious displays. 'Nearly lost the match with your little exhibition.'

I had paid no attention to the small wiry man, perched

high on his umpire's chair. He introduced himself as Jock. His face was weathered from years outdoors and his legs bowed beneath his white shorts. He was in front of me before I dared speak. 'Perhaps I need to learn some discipline.' Although still unsure, I tossed my head insolently.

No sooner had I spoken than he yanked away my towel and revealed the metal belt. He stared at it lewdly and produced the silver key from his pocket. He released the padlock easily and snapped up the shield before he pulled me towards the slatted bench that ran the length of the room and spanked me soundly. I have never been chastised before, except by you. He aimed carefully, pausing between blows, but with irregular intervals, prolonging my pain and shame. When he was done he led me across to his caretaker's cottage. He hung the belt, like a trophy, beside a picture of himself as a sergeant-major, the peak of his cap tipped low over his brow. I hardly slept that night on the mattress he slung on the kitchen floor, tormented by your cruelty.

The coaching sessions began at dawn before even the keenest members arrived and continued when the club closed at night. In spite of his wizened frame, Jock was a consummate player, aiming the balls precisely, forcing me to lunge awkwardly around the court until he called me to the net and ordered me to bend over it. He raised my skirt and pulled down my knickers while barking disparagements at my ineptitude. I grasped the netting, ready for the spanking I anticipated. But when he lifted his racquet in the air, all I could do was wait for the inevitable thud of the leather-bound handle as it met my buttocks.

Those days with Jock, while he drilled me like a young

soldier in his command, were so hard. One evening, he removed my shirt to observe my serve better and when I didn't reach high enough, he unfastened my bra and attached weights to my nipples. I blinked back my tears but my stoicism earned me no mercy. After that, he took away my underwear so that I was constantly exposed to his leers. Sometimes he fastened me to the struts of his umpire's chair and groped me with his calloused hands. I tolerated his intrusions into my body but it gave me no pleasure and he punished me for my denial with his racquet, a branch from the overhanging trees or the flat of his huge palm. My days were spent locked in the cottage unless he took me to the locker room, tied me on my back to the slatted bench and between his other duties, came to sneer at my fear of discovery. One afternoon, he brought a woman. She was in her forties with a handsome, horsey face. She looked down at me mockingly before lifting my skirt to tease between my parted thighs. When she found my clitoris, my mortification was complete.

But although she gloated over the beating I received for succumbing to her delving touch, I am grateful to her. As my orgasm seeped through me, Jock turned me and used his belt to thrash me. And, as you have taught me to absorb the pain, so under the slicing cuts of leather, the surges built for a second time.

That afternoon signalled my surrender. I stopped struggling for control when he beat me and let the throbbing heat well inside me. I let him gratify me with his gnarled fingers and punish my lust, until my mind confused the two and I no longer resisted either. For a while he enjoyed my hankering descent as I accepted his regime but I suspect his real satisfaction comes from dismantling the resistance of those in his charge. Yesterday, he reapplied my chastity belt and released me.

Now I am alone again in my studio, struggling with new discoveries, unable to assuage my longing for you while the shield prevents it. By now, Jock will have returned the key. Will you send for me and release me now, my love?

Leo shut down his laptop and looked out at the teaming bustle of the Tokyo night. He had been awaiting the arrival of her letter since Jock had called to report her release. Now he longed to pick up the phone and hear her voice, sleepy and warm with desire. But he resisted and let his mind fill with thoughts of the old soldier arousing and punishing her. His second letter would reach her in a few hours and it was too late to prevent it.

This evening you will attend a concert at a private house. Again, you must seek the person who holds the key and find your deepest recesses of HUMILITY. When you have learned the lesson, you must write to me again.

I confess, I wept when I received your new instructions. I thought that my time with Jock was proof enough. The house in Mayfair was imposing and elegantly designed. The other guests chatted as we were taken through to the music room. A silk-draped ceiling hung from a central pillar and exotic rugs were strewn in the style of an Eastern tent. The audience of about thirty people seated themselves on the sumptuous couches and embroidered cushions. Our host, Peter, a distinguished man in his fifties with a shock of silver hair, guided me to a low stool and sat beside me. As soon as the cellist raised her bow, I guessed it was him. His thigh stiffened against my green silk dress – the one you bought for me in Milan. In spite of the way it clung to my hips, the chastity belt was hidden beneath it. Schubert's melodies helped to calm my nerves, as did the wine I gulped when we gathered in the adjoining salon, before I dared approach him. He enquired how I had enjoyed the music and I talked loquaciously about a superior performance I had attended.

'You demonstrate the arrogance of youth,' he retorted.

'Perhaps it needs tempering?' I responded.

He waited until I blushed under the scrutiny of his glare. 'Go to the music room and wait.'

Thirty minutes later, he strode into the room. I had little time to compose myself before his hand reached for the neckline of my dress. With one sharp jerk, he ripped the delicate silk from neck to hem. Beneath it, I was naked except for the thin steel glinting in the candlelight, accentuating my pubic mound. He produced the key with a flourish and let his hands brush against my protruding lips while he skilfully removed the device. Wordlessly, he pushed me down on the cushions and held my neck to receive my first spanking. Jock's tutelage had released my inhibitions and added to the recent removal of the shield, the floodgates opened under his practiced hand and I betrayed myself quickly. My moans masked the entrance of the woman and it wasn't until he'd hauled me trembling to my feet that he introduced his sister, Margaret. I recognised her angular features instantly as the woman Jock had brought to the changing room.

'I'll take her tonight,' she stated haughtily. She took me upstairs to her rooms, furnished to her more Victorian taste, and made me grasp the bedpost while she laced me into a whalebone corset. It left my ribs and waist encased and my breasts exposed and I panted for breath as she buckled a heavy collar around my neck. That is how I remained trussed throughout my stay there.

From then on they passed me between them, colluding in their methods to degrade me. Often Margaret would send me downstairs with a note detailing my misdemeanours, and Peter would dictate my punishment. If I was forced to wake him, my chastisement was the greater. He kept a selection of whips, canes and tawses and took time, while I crouched on the end of his leash, to choose. Often he lashed me to the central pillar in the music room and used his favourite – a vicious cat-o'-nine-tails. The leather thongs licked up between the crack in my buttocks and stung my tenderest skin. If I derived any pleasure from it, he turned me and brought the tails down between my parted gash, whipping the hardening berry. When he drove the thick studded handle into either orifice, he watched me gasp, his thin lips twisting cruelly.

Upstairs, Margaret treated me as her servant, always on my knees. And whenever she desired, she raised her skirts and jerked on my leash, compelling me to seek out her swelling clitoris. One afternoon, she held a bridge party for her female friends. I was made to crouch beneath the table and pleasure whoever was designated *dummy* for the hand. I should have felt more humbled by my task but I confess that I found the anonymous lips enthralling and pride in hearing the tight gasps of release as they succumbed to my tongue.

But there was no anonymity on the last night when they finally annulled my vanity. I heard the guests arriving. 'A *special* concert tonight,' Margaret breathed huskily, her eyes bright with anticipation as she tightened the laces of my corset.

How can I describe the humiliation as the recital began, of being made to crawl between their groping hands? And to be required to service whoever lifted their dress or opened their trousers, their juices mingling in my mouth, soaking my cheeks and breasts? To have a woman pinch my nipples while her husband rams his length down my throat or thrust her fingers into me and use my juices to lubricate herself?

When the music ended, Peter took me to the stage and blindfolded me. He laid me face down on the long piano stool and offered the men a choice of implements. He held my shoulders while he allowed each man three strikes, to be alternated with the women pleasuring me. The first beatings felt sharp – the thwack of a cane – a wide tawse slapping my buttocks apart – and the women, competing with their mouths and hands. But as they turned me over and over, faster and faster, and my orgasms collided and converged with the heavy blows, every sense was opened until my disembodied voice begged incoherently for more. Until I relinquished all resistance and was purged of every boundary – until I sank into a well of consciousness.

Oh Leo. To know you sanctioned such a public degradation is hard but as I begged, I found a place beyond my conscious self. Peter secured my chastity belt before he released me and once again I am unable to soothe my longing. Will you be home soon, my love?

Leo finished reading and clicked the remote. Beth's image writhing, blindfolded on the piano stool appeared on the screen. Peter had done well. The tape had been waiting when he arrived in New York. He watched it again, engrossed in her ascent into the unhindered world where pain and pleasure fuse. One final test. The hardest one of all – for both of them. He wiped the sweat from his brow, suddenly uneasy.

I have returned the key to you. This evening you will go to a night club and confront the UNKNOWN. You will dress provocatively and hand the key to your guide, yourself. And whatever events unfold, you must describe to me.

In spite of your directions, it was a difficult place to find, hidden beneath the arches in South London and the smell of female sweat overpowered me as I entered its cave-like interior. I tottered uncertainly towards the bar on my stiletto heels. A heavy woman in a plaid shirt was the first to buy me a drink. Soon I was encircled by others, similarly dressed, squeezing predatorily against me and I was pleased that, beneath my short skirt, the metal shield offered me protection. The club was packed but every eye turned when Evelyn appeared in the doorway. She was dressed in a tailored evening suit and her hair cut into a sleek, mannish bob that framed her perfect oval face. She sensed new blood at once and the crowd parted with unspoken abeyance to allow her a clear view.

I was so sure that you had sent her that when she tapped her silver-topped cane on the floor, I followed her from the club like a puppy. As soon as we arrived at her airy loft apartment, she undressed me. Her eyes widened when she saw the metal guard and the padlock that secured it and wider still when she saw the marks that still criss-crossed my body. I expected her to reach for the key, nestling openly between my breasts and remove the belt to spank me as her predecessors had done. But instead she laid me on her bed and caressed me until I ached with shameless need and begged her to use the key to release me.

'One day, you will ask for its return,' she whispered as she undid the padlock and placed it, with the device, in her desk drawer. That night, we made love until dawn and I discovered uncharted depths in another woman's arms. When I woke, she was writing at her desk, lit by a shaft of morning sun from the skylight. She carried me to the bathroom and rubbed ointment into my blemishes. When she'd bathed me, she fed me and lifted me into bed, while she continued working. And that became the pattern of our lives. She asked no questions and tended to my every need. I was never out of her sight. Even in the bathroom, she would knead my stomach while I emptied myself and I craved her attentions and hated the times she ignored me, absorbed by her writing.

But as time passed, she began to torture me. She stayed longer at her desk and became perfunctory in her care of me. Try as I did to please her, nothing brought back our joyful passion. My frustration grew as I became her prisoner, more trapped than the belt has ever rendered me, deprived of my work – but unable to summon the will to leave. At night, she still rolled her tongue around my clitoris, peeling back the hood until the raw bud swelled and drove me into white ecstasy. But as my pleasure subsided she turned away, leaving me bereft. Until at last I couldn't bear another moment of her heartlessness and begged her to return the key.

'Then you must earn it!' Her eyes flashed with the same fervour I have seen in yours.

The following morning, I awoke to find my ankles fastened to the bed by thin chains. Several hours later she returned, laden with packages. Before she unpacked her purchases, she cleaned and fed me with all the affection she had shown in our early days.

The ropes she slung over the high wooden beams were strong enough to bear my weight in any position she devised. While she worked, she kept me doubled above her and I endured the pain in my limbs, longing for the times she broke off and sought inspiration by plunging her fist into the heat of my body. When my orgasm exploded, she beat me with a short bamboo cane which she kept ready on her desk. She became fascinated in finding new ways to punish me and devoted all our evenings to that pursuit. But afterwards, she would take me to her bed and kiss away the pain she had inflicted, stroking the heat out of my burning buttocks, leading us both into relentless rapture.

Until last week, after she bathed me, instead of fastening me to the rafters, she took the chastity belt from her desk and fitted it securely. When she had locked it she offered me the key, the slightest frown being the only clue to her emotions. How do I explain this to you, Leo? Before we kissed goodbye, I hung it lovingly around her neck.

It felt good to be back in my studio, sketching with new-found freedom. But as the light faded, I was drawn to return to her and she was waiting to unlock the belt and punish me for my absence. Last night she had fitted a pulley to the skylight to which she fastened my wrists, with dumbbells around my ankles so she could move them at will. She selected a plaited crop and made me ask and thank her six times, ensuring each cut crossed the last, until I was striped to her satisfaction. She showed more zeal than ever and our passion afterwards was the greater for it. But as I lay in her arms, I knew the time had come to make my choice.

This morning, after she had fitted the chastity belt, I took the silver key from around her neck and left her.

Leo looked at his watch and paced the marble floor. He'd been home for a month and not a word, until now. His initial anxiety had turned to anger and frustration. Had the *UNKNOWN* proved his undoing? He regretted that he hadn't selected his own guide for her final trial. Now he feared this rival for her affections – yet he was intrigued by this female seducer with a mind so like his own.

Beth cleaned her brushes and considered her *surrender* under Jock's tutelage and her *humility* at the whim of the two siblings. But as she uncorked his favourite burgundy, it was the consequences of the *unknown* that concerned her. She continued to arrange the tray of glasses as the door opened behind her.

'We're expecting company, I see,' he said stiffly. A passing train delayed her need to respond but as it faded she turned to see Evelyn step into the studio behind Leo.

Beth smiled to herself as she poured. Punctuality was another attribute they shared.

Beth sipped her wine, adding to the tension dancing between them, but Leo drank deeply, anxious for an early outcome to this charged encounter. A smile of triumph lit his handsome face as he tossed back the dregs and caught the silver key between his teeth. His doubts evaporated and he stepped forward confidently to claim her. It took all her strength to resist his embrace.

Evelyn looked away and put down her glass to leave, her hurt visible.

'Finish your drink,' Beth said softly, 'Please?'

Evelyn mustered every ounce of dignity and raised her glass. Leo turned to watch his adversary, just as she opened her mouth wide and the point of her tongue emerged – an identical silver key glinting in it.

'I had a duplicate cut this morning,' Beth's heart quickened as she waited for her two lovers to digest her words.

Leo was the first to raise his glass. He smiled slowly. 'To the Unknown?'

'To the Unknown,' Evelyn's voice was edged with a new expectation.

How alike they were – how could she relinquish either one of them?

Beth sighed with happiness as their glasses met to seal their union and let her skirt drop to the floor, revealing the chastity belt clinging to the contours of her body, ready to be unlocked.

Think Pink

Bruce Anderson

*A**NY moment now he'd be thrashing the pertest bottom in Britain.* Darren stared at Suzie Starr as the strains of Duran Duran's *Planet Earth* filled her villa. The pilot of *Salvage With Suzie* was about to begin.

Facing the cameras, Suzie started off with her customary confidence. 'I'm Suzie Starr and over the next eight weeks I'll show you how to recycle and reuse hundreds of everyday items. Together we'll replenish the environment.' The camera following, she walked into her dressing room and pointed to three pairs of bootcut jeans. 'Don't throw out yesterday's fashions – donate them to charity shops.' Holding up a worn dress, she added 'And take older outfits to the Clothing Bank for recycling. They can be shredded and used for insulation or to stuff mattresses.'

'She's good,' Darren's production assistant murmured.

'Trust me, she's about to be very bad,' Darren said.

Following the rehearsed script, Suzie glided into the kitchen and examined a container of wilting salad leaves. 'Never throw decomposing food in the dustbin – compost it!' Arse a perfect peach in clingy black jeans, she wiggled her way to her palatial lounge and joined Darren on the settee. 'Now, I like curling up on the couch with an organic cocoa as much as the next girl – but for the next five minutes I'm going to be curling up with our producer Darren Scott, author of the bestseller *Ending World*.'

The world as she knew it was also about to end. Darren smiled as he sat down next to her. 'Suzie, as you doubtless know, there are millions of households which say that they've gone green when they've only made token changes to their lifestyle.'

'I've noticed that, too, Darren,' Suzie murmured, shaking her pretty blonde bob. 'But tokenism isn't good enough. We have to cut consumption and go organic on a large scale if our planet is to survive.'

'Which is why,' Darren said, 'we've decided to go behind the scenes here in your lovely home so that we can show viewers the endless ways you're saving the environment.'

He smiled inwardly as he heard Suzie's alarmed gasp. For the first time he'd deviated from the script, rendering her speechless. 'Let's check out more than these lettuce leaves,' he said, taking a firm hold of her arm and marching her back to the kitchen, the wheeled camera in hot pursuit.

He opened the fridge and brought out four apples on a pre-packaged tray.

'Where did these come from?'

'Tesco,' Suzie said lamely.

'South Africa,' Darren amended, checking the label. 'We're at the height of the English apple season yet you're blatantly squandering carbon miles on foreign fruit.' He took out a carton of eggs. 'These aren't free-range – in other words, you've let birds be debeaked and caged for life so that you can save a few pence.'

'I… can we please stop filming?' Suzie asked, looking pleadingly at the camera man.

Darren nodded with pretend regret. 'We might as well – after all, we want a genuine environmentalist. You told us at the audition that you lived a green life.'

'I do,' Suzie said, her blue eyes wide. 'It's just that I've had such a busy schedule.'

Darren shook his head. 'You've no schedule, haven't worked since *I'm A Nonentity, Get Me Out Of Here*.'

'I… took a career break but now my agent's sifting through offers for me,' Suzie stammered.

'Then you'd best take one of them. You're all wrong for us.'

'Isn't there any way…?'

He almost yelped as Suzie stepped closer and slid her hand over his crotch. Taking a deep breath, he composed himself. 'I suppose you could wipe the slate clean by taking a damn good spanking.'

To his amazement, she said 'Done.' He'd forgotten, just for a nano-second, how desperate most failing celebs were – they'd starve, lie, snort and fuck to retain a vestige of their former fame.

He turned to the camera man. 'Brian, set up the camera in Suzie's bedroom then bugger off down the pub. I'll phone you on your mobile when we're ready to resume.'

'You're filming me being spanked?' Suzie asked, blushing hotly.

'Just for my own delectation.'

'And afterwards I get to make the pilot?'

Darren flexed his palm. 'It's guaranteed.'

To his amazement, she took his hand in her own damp palm and led him to her bedroom where Brian was already training the camera on her King Size divan.

'Bye,' Darren said gruffly.

'You lucky bastard,' Brian said.

He left. Darren sat down on the edge of the bed and patted his lap. 'Come here.'

His groin pulsed as Suzie hastened to obey him. She was surprisingly light – he calculated less than eight stone – as she settled her weight across his thighs.

For a few moments, Darren contented himself with stroking her small, oval buttocks through her jeans, enjoying her mortification.

'What a bad girl you've been,' he murmured, 'so very wilful. Did you know that not one of the cleaning products in your kitchen is toxin-free?'

'But ethical products cost more and now that the work's dried up…' Suzie gasped.

'Old fashioned elbow grease doesn't.'

'I have to keep my hands soft in case I find work.'

'In other words, the planet dies so that you can look pretty,' Darren said, raising his right hand and bringing it down hard on her bouncing little backside. To his delight, she squealed and squirmed across his erection. He kept his hand busy with a regular tattoo throughout the warm up session, preparing her for the much harder spanking, and caning, she'd have to endure.

'It's time that these came down,' he said at last, reaching under her and locating the metal button and zip. To his surprise, she raised up to help him. Could she actually enjoy being spanked, he wondered. He wanted to punish her for her many sins, not give her an erotic experience!

'No one's ever done this before,' she muttered as he edged the black denim over her arse.

'You surprise me.' Three years before, at the height of her fame, she'd slapped one of the paparazzi, insulted a rival daytime presenter and – the worst sin of all – gained half a stone whilst filming *Starr Suppers*. The industry had begun to avoid her, though she'd gotten some mileage out of making *Slim Down With Suzie* after losing ten pounds. But she was twenty-six now, a dinosaur in celebrity terms, and they were chasing the latest teenage temptress instead.

He stripped her of her designer blouse, fretwork bra and jeans but to his disappointment she wasn't wearing any panties. Whenever he'd fantasised about spanking her, she'd always worn lots of layers which could be humiliatingly raised or pulled slowly down. Sometimes he'd edge down her shorts and discipline her bare bottom with his hand then re-dress her in his imagination so that he could lift her skirt and underskirt and give her a follow-up thrashing – with a paddle – that she'd never forget.

'No panties?' he murmured now.

'I didn't want to risk Visible Panty Line,' Suzie explained, wriggling.

'Of course you didn't.' He turned his attention to her radiant rear, enjoying its pinkness and the heat that communicated itself to his caressing palm. 'It's going to hurt a lot more now that I've taken your jeans off,' he added conversationally.

He heard her sharp intake of breath, saw her hide her face in her arms. Hoisting her more firmly across his lap, he began to lash her naked contours. He slapped for all the times she'd taken part in some stupid show with an alliterative title. He slapped to punish her for contributing to dumbed-down TV. He watched dispassionately as she jerked and kicked and implored him, as she desperately tried to rise up and push his fingers away.

She weighed less than eight stone, he weighed thirteen. There was no contest. She'd doubtless had a yolk-free omelette for breakfast whereas he'd enjoyed the full monty and coffee with cream. He slapped strongly at her reddening flesh, enjoying her entreaties and half-yelps. Though his hard palm was smarting, her soft flesh was stinging much, much more.

'Please stop,' she gasped out, 'I can't take it.'

'You mean you don't want to make the pilot?' he asked sadly. He stayed his spanking hand then tossed her down on the bed.

'No, I do!' Holding her flaming buttocks, she rolled onto her side and stared up at him beseechingly.

'Well, the pact was that I punish you for your numerous environmental indiscretions. I've hardly started and you're welshing on the deal.'

'I know, but… I'd no idea it would hurt this much.'

'You're destroying the planet and expect to get off with a couple of taps?'

'I guess not.'

'Ask me nicely to continue spanking you,' Darren said.

He stared as she swallowed hard, still protectively cupping her scarlet bottom.

'A sound thrashing or TV oblivion – it's your choice,' he explained.

'You'd better be on the level,' Suzie muttered. She

inhaled visibly then wriggled her way back onto his lap.

This time she cried out from the very first spank and tried desperately to protect her punished foundation. Stopping briefly, Darren took off his tie and bound her hands in front of her, ignoring her suggestion that she could please him with her hand. Now that her protective palms were out of the way, he had an uninterrupted view of a fingermarked canvas, a canvas where he would make his mark again and again.

At last his hand tired and he rolled her fully onto the mattress. 'Let's take a closer look around your apartment, check out any other indiscretions, Miss Starr.'

'My hands…' She held out her captive wrists to him in a supplicating gesture.

'Oh, we'll better leave them tied,' Darren said lightly, 'I haven't finished today's lesson yet.'

He watched her swallow hard. 'You haven't?'

With mock regret, he shook his head. 'I reckon I'm about halfway through teaching you the error of your ways.'

'If you untie me, I promise not to protect myself,' Suzie said, looking up at him hopefully.

'You would,' Darren assured her, remembering all of the wanabees he'd caned earlier in the year whilst casting for *Go Organic*. No matter how fervently a girl proffered her naked buttocks, her hands always flew to them when the cane lashed down. 'Let's check out the bathroom,' he added, knowing that most women kept numerous toxic products there. As he'd suspected, she was no exception. 'Oh dear – your skincare is full of SLS parabens and you're…' He shuddered for effect, 'using an aerosol deodorant rather than a deo-crystal for your underarms.'

'Tell me what to use and I'll use it,' Suzie whispered, her breasts heaving as she breathed hard and fast. Her face was hectic.

'It's my duty to thrash the message into you with my cane,' Darren replied, reading label after label in her cluttered bathroom and sadly shaking his head.

'Your cane? You only mentioned a spanking.'

'Spanking with a hand then with a cane. It's the only way to drive the message home,' he said casually.

He watched as the presenter gulped several times and looked wildly around the bathroom. 'But I'm already so tender.'

'The pain of the spanking will have faded by tomorrow whereas a good thrashing with a cane reminds a naughty girl of her errors for many days.' He examined her feminine care products. 'Oh Suzie, these are chlorine-bleached.'

'I'm going to do *so* much better,' the naked blonde said, her scarlet bottom twitching nervously.

'To the kitchen next, I think,' Darren said, making her walk before him down the stairs. Her backside was so taut that it hardly jiggled. To his pretend-consternation he found that she wasn't recycling this week's copies of *Closer*, *Heat*, *OK* or *Hello* and had also binned two wine bottles and ten fruit-cocktail cans, despite having a council salvage bin in her utility room.

'Could do better,' Suzie mumbled, her arse puckering strongly.

'Should taste the cane and completely reform,' Darren replied.

'Can't I at least put my jeans back on?' Suzie pleaded.

'No, I like to mark a completely bare bottom, admire

my handiwork,' Darren said. Taking her elbow, he steered her into the lounge and positioned her at the end of the couch then bent her gently over until her buttocks were raised high in the air. 'Stretch your tied hands far out in front of you,' he said. 'Further... That's it.' The arrangement helped to elevate her arse to its fullest whilst making it hard for her to rise up or shield herself in any way.

'Let's get the rod nicely lined up.' He took his time, bouncing it ever so lightly against her firmament, watching her quake.

'What if I can't take it?' Suzie whispered.

He indicated his briefcase, tucked discreetly in the alcove. 'Then we could try you with a nice hard wooden paddle or swishy riding crop instead.'

But the cane was his own personal favourite so he stood back and flicked it with moderate force into her rump and she cried out and raised up slightly, using her bound arms as awkward leverage. But he was ready for her and helped her back into place.

'Just take deep breaths, think of the upside – the fee, the acclaim, all these newspaper interviews. Chances are you'll make the cover of the environmental magazines.'

He watched as she underwent an inner battle, her arse begging for release, her brain demanding that she take her punishment. Eventually her brain won and she settled herself more heavily on the couch and uttered a tremulous 'Please get it over with.'

'Oh a caning can't be rushed,' Darren explained, gently stroking the glowing mark already left by his swishy rod. 'The backside in question has to reflect on its mistakes, has to fear the next stripe of retribution.'

'I fear it,' the blonde said with feeling, and he could see that she was finding it hard to keep her feverish little bottom in place.

'You're right to fear it – the first cut is only the deepest in sentimental songs.' He raised the rattan and applied it to the flesh immediately below the existing tramline. Suzie howled.

'Third time lucky?' the producer asked with satisfaction when she at last stopped jerking around.

'What do you mean?' Suzie whispered.

'Well, if you're lucky I'll miss the tendermost area where arse meets thigh.' He lined the punisher up with that particular area then applied it smartly. 'Oops.'

'No more!' Suzie said, jumping to her feet, tugging wildly at her hands and stamping her feet on the spot as she tried to wiggle the pain away.

It was time for another heart to heart – well, palm to bottom. Taking a seat on the couch, he hauled her over his knee and began to caress her heated flesh.

'You're halfway there. You don't want to blow it now.'

'I could blow you instead,' Suzie murmured.

He thought about it for a second. 'No, I'd rather finish re-educating your bare backside.'

'But it hurts so much,' she wailed with what sounded like a genuine cry in her voice.

'What about the pain that you've caused to factory-farmed chickens? The dolphins which died in nets because you didn't insist on ethical tuna-fishing? The rabbits blinded by your beauty products and shampoos?'

She twisted her head back to look piteously at him. 'I'm so sorry about all of that. You know I'll change!'

'You'll definitely change after six of the best,' Darren

said. He helped her to her feet. 'And, because I'm a kind man, I'm going to administer the last three strokes in the garden where the breeze will cool your naughty buttocks down.'

Somewhat to his surprise, she didn't voice any complaint as he marched her out to the back lawn which was surrounded by a six foot high brick wall on all sides. In his fantasies – and in reality whenever he could get away with it – he did some of his most erotic punishing outside.

He looked thoughtfully around the large, square space. One corner contained a water butt which, upon closer inspection, had never been used.

'A water butt to hoist a bad butt – how appropriate,' he murmured, turning the container on its side and bending her over it, her bound palms and bare soles of feet scraping the concrete path.

'If my gardener appears, I'll die of embarrassment,' Suzie mumbled.

'If your gardener appears, I'll get him to hold you in place,' Darren said.

He lined up the rod then applied it to the upper part of her arse, taking care to concentrate on the fleshy areas. Taken by surprise, she almost rolled over the butt.

'Silly girl, keep that bad bottom in place for me.' He took his time positioning her, palming her flaming buttocks, enjoying her frenzied wriggling. These last strokes were for all the times she'd lied to the cameras, pretending that her good looks were effortless or that she was naturally thin. Half of the image-obsessed and anorexic teenagers in Britain had probably been influenced by the likes of Suzie Starr.

With relish, he laid the fifth stroke in place, though she jerked at the last minute and the rattan landed diagonally rather than straight across. 'If you keep wriggling, I'm going to get angry,' he warned, 'And you really don't want that.'

Belatedly he remembered that he'd left the camera in the bedroom, told her that he was going to fetch it.

'These pictures better not end up on the internet,' she said in a muffled voice.

'Trust me, they'll only end up on my bedroom computer.' He had two dozen such disks, of everything from wanabee rock chicks to fading daytime presenters, all being caned and shamed before offering him sexual satisfaction. They'd do almost anything to gain the Mercedes, the penthouse, the admiring fans – and they'd do even more to avoid losing it.

The adrenaline flowing through his veins, he hurried into the house then saw her digital camera lying beside her PC. That would do for a final memento. Walking smartly back, he focused on her dependent backside.

It was a beautiful sight, and one he relished, her arse an all-over red from the earlier spanking. This glowing canvas was overwritten by the deeper, darker tramlines caused by the cane. He could see all five of his splendid efforts, and felt a momentary regret that he'd have to stop at six.

'Say cheese,' he joked, though her face was turned away from him. She muttered something which sounded like 'fuck you' and he gave an admonishing slap to her bare backside. She howled and squirmed about on the green plastic barrel, her bottom looking like it wanted to launch itself into space. 'Only one to go,' he said with mock reassurance. 'Now where should I put it? Here or here or here?' As he spoke, he bounced the rattan thoughtfully against her crimson contours until she begged him to put her out of her misery.

'I think we'll aim for the halfway mark,' he said at last, then stopped and put down the cane. 'But first I must take a photo of your face. Such a pretty picture.' Walking around to the front, he knelt down and snapped her flushed cheeks and tear-filled eyes. He'd make her a printout of this snap so that she could look at it whenever she was tempted to be hypocritical, to lead impressionable youth astray.

'And we'll make the pilot after this?' Suzie asked, wincing as she rolled more fully forward and her naked nipples rubbed against the ground.

'Uh huh. I doubt if you'll want to sit down for the rest of the day, so I'll come back tomorrow. You can do all your environmental shopping tonight.'

'And you'll give me a list of what to buy?' Suzie added tremulously, 'I so want to get this right.'

'Oh you will – your sore arse will remind you to read all the books, to examine every label. And every time that you're tempted to take short cuts, you'll remember the feel of my cane lashing down.' He picked up the rattan and returned to her rear view. 'Talking of which...'

By now, she was clearly in an agony of anticipation, desperate to accept the last searing stroke yet dreading its arrival. As such, she jerked about like the proverbial cat on a hot tin roof. And it *was* hot out here, Darren thought, the cooling breeze he'd offered having failed to materialise. Instead, the August sun beat down on her bare buttocks, adding to their heat.

'Almost done,' he said with genuine regret. Flexing the cane between his hands, he decided to enliven her susceptible underswell. He laid on the rod with moderate force and she yelled and almost overshot the water butt again.

Putting her over his shoulder in a fireman's lift, he carried her back to the bedroom, laid her across his lap and examined his handiwork.

'No more,' she said, 'Oh please!'

'I promised you six of the best, and six you've had,' Darren murmured, kneading her vanquished nates. 'Tomorrow we start filming.'

'Ah! Ouch! Ow! I promise to be the perfect presenter,' Suzie said.

'There's also a World Environmental Day special being planned for next June,' Darren added. 'And we haven't chosen a presenter yet. But my cock's so hard that I can't think…'

'I could help you think,' Suzie whispered on cue, putting her manicured hand on his fly.

'Well, if you insist, a nice tongue bath always wakes me up,' Darren replied, closing his eyes as she unzipped him. He opened them wide when he felt her mouth closing over his rod. She was kneeling between his legs and sucking avidly at his hardness, her reddened bottom quivering as she moved her head. It was the horniest thing he'd seen for some time, the producer admitted to himself, and he was no stranger to erotic encounters. But there was something special about being fellated by every teenage boy's wet dream. And the fact that he'd just toasted her backside made it extra special, as did the fact that he knew she'd eventually slip up again.

Oh, the reformed Suzie wanted to go green, and she'd be motivated for as long as she was filming this new series. But, a few weeks from now, she'd forget to recycle her toner cartridge or would be tempted into buying some eco-unfriendly mangoes or an increasingly-scarce variety of fish. And he'd pop round for a surprise visit and discover her indiscretions and she'd end up, kicking and screaming, over his knee. He knew that she'd acquiesce – after all, he held the carrot of that Environmental Day special. She wouldn't want to miss out on such prestigious and high profile work.

Darren cried out as he came strongly in her mouth, then smiled inwardly as he looked forward to future sessions. He flexed his spanking arm: Suzie might be going green but he was looking forward to thinking pink.

Rubious – The Colour of Rubies

Mark Ramsden

I was a teenage Satanist, a black-eyed bad girl with blood red teeth.

In other words I was a shy Goth, a Sylvia Plath fan, a pale, thin brunette sealed in black. Red was my second favourite colour, particularly the shade of soundly smacked bottoms. Cane lines crayoned on white flesh. Red passion flowers. Or perhaps it was the canvas on which they were etched. Artists need a flat casel but those who work on flesh prefer curves. This sort of work should be done as slowly as possible, preferably on chubby buttocks, the sort one must fondle before, during and after a punishment. Just to ascertain whether the skin can take any more reddening, of course. One wouldn't want to besmirch the noble art of chastisement with sexuality. At least not until the receiver has been allowed to rub their bottom, perhaps while pouting defiantly, and after they have spread themselves in whatever position in which they like to receive oral sex. Or something a little more invasive…

My teenage hobbies were mooching around and deciding how suicidal I was. Usually while reading Sylvia Plath. I would wonder who would miss me after I was gone. How much I could hurt them. How they would rue the day they upset *me*, the centre of the known universe.

Perhaps I just needed someone to thrash some sense into me, fortunately I met a wise older woman. Her name was also Sylvia, although, unlike Plath, there was nothing remotely masochistic about her. She taught me the benefits of a sound scourging on a moonlit night. Black clothes, red wine, white moon, scarlet bottoms and shared sighs – we were the cruel sisters, taking it in turns to whip each other into a frenzy. I was fond of my teacher. She whipped me well. She showed me how to make money from my passion, helping me to become a pro-Domme. She even taught me new words to describe a beating, sometimes over her knee, with one spank for each letter.

'Vapulation' – an obscure word for flogging – how it hurt memorising *that* one! 'Rubious' was another one of Sylvia's obscure words, one that would drive any Scrabble opponent into a red mist rage. It took fewer smacks to learn that one, perhaps because 'the colour of rubies' was poetic enough to be memorable.

Now I'm on my fourth twenty-ninth birthday I still persevere with men. Heaven knows why, as they're mostly *useless*. But I much prefer spanking women. And the most recent jewel in my crown was Svetlana, a Russian mafia princess.

She came into my life when I was looking for someone to kill my ex-husband. Too much information? Well, it was only a passing phase. I'd rather have him alive these days. That way he'll suffer much longer.

Geezer Hardnut, my boyfriend, when I can prise him away from the Playstation, arranged for me to meet Svetlana. She was a genuine female assassin. So he said. He might be a liar but he's killed more people than I have so I have to go with it. Particularly as I spent at least a year wanting my ex-husband killed. I admit I may have lost a little perspective when they took my children away from me. Actually, I never got as far as discussing my husband's disposal with Svetlana. Some film noir heroine I would have made.

Svetlana was my scarlet woman. You could use 'rubious' to describe her crimson lipstick and the broken veins in her bloodshot eyes. It was also the colour of her pert little bum once I had finished paddling it. Svetlana was thin, chic, adorably scatty and most probably insane. Her skin was as white as the paper I write on, her bruises as black as my ink. Like my teenage self, Svetlana wore only black and red. Black boots, red leather mini-skirt. Her conversation also had one theme: what she wanted next. Apart from her blonde hair this was going to be like spanking my teenage self.

'You talk too much! Beat me! I want to be *flogged*. Flogged hard!'

Typical Svetlana. She can't even be bothered to wait for a proper introduction. I can hear her husky voice, too loud from vodka and smoky from too many cigarettes. 'Linear narrative? Is for *pussies*! Pull my knickers down and smack my bottom!. *Hard*!'

Well. If you *insist*.

We had a few quick drinks, the quickest I had ever

had. Then I knew I wasn't hiring her as a hitwoman. You can't trust chronic alcoholics. Especially not when they have a bad cold in mid-summer and a need to visit the bathroom every ten minutes. But you can still seduce them. As soon as we were back at my place we kissed till our lips hurt. I dragged her over my knee. One of her hands found the floor while the other grasped my foot tightly. She started to kiss my ankles. I slowly eased her white lace panties down. I was sopping wet just from the sight of her firm, chubby rump.

'Lay still, my girl,' I told her. 'You're going to get the spanking of a life time.'

She had no more hope of laying still than a landed fish gasping for air. I smacked her hard as she wriggled and sighed. I caressed her, fingering her openings, patting her firm, fleshy cheeks. As the heat built up she moaned loudly but she wasn't going to beg for mercy.

They don't spare the rod in Russia. She was probably used to having her pretty little bottom striped hard. And she was drunk enough to take a lot of pain. After a while my hand was hurting too much.

Her bottom was red and glowing, yet still ripe for more punishment. Despite the pain she still managed to stick it out and up. Before continuing I took a moment to contemplate the seat of pain and pleasure, the site of pride and shame. It was the finest specimen I had ever had at my disposal. Much too good to rush.

'I keep this heart-shaped paddle for those I love,' I said, picking up my favourite implement. I watched her closely, looking to see if the word love terrified her. It often does. Because who needs another needy stalker? After a certain age the fiction of a mystic other or perfect lover can no longer sustain us. Luckily our needs and desires remain as fierce as ever, perhaps even more so with the realisation that there is less time in which to indulge our desires.

'Who cares who you love?' she gasped, 'Hit me!'

It was the right answer I suppose. Certainly the one to get her bottom smacked as quickly as possible. I unleashed a quick flurry of spanks. Which gave her something to think about. And then I told myself off for losing control.

I usually ask a receiver to kiss the paddle before and after use. Sometimes I douse the surface with water because it makes an already tender bottom much more sensitive to the smacking leather impact. And because moist reddening cheeks look even more enticing. I asked her to kiss the paddle, already slightly warm from contact with her hot bottom. Then I laid it to one side and picked my tawse up.

This'll make you tingle, you hard-arsed bitch. I gave her three quick, hard whacks. She screamed and begged me to stop. Finally! I was getting somewhere. She reached a hand behind her to block my access but, like any mother since time immemorial I merely grabbed the hand and jammed it further up her back. I raised my left thigh to position her more temptingly. She rewarded my efforts by sprawling lewdly, showing me her shaven pout and releasing more of the scent that drives me wild: freshly spanked, horny young woman. I never tire of it.

I dangled the tawse between her legs, rubbing it back and forth as she opened further for me. I smacked her bottom harder. I used the tip of my middle finger right on her puckered little anus and shoved two of my fingers in her mouth. She sucked on them greedily, eager to show me she would now do anything. Her bottom was red hot to the touch.

'Had enough darling?'

'You call this pain? In Russia we *birch* each other.'

Bloody cheek! This is sometimes called bratting. Behaving as a bratt to provoke punishment. Some find it cute. I find it annoying but a pretty bottom excuses a multitude of sins.

'Really?' I said. 'I wonder if you have sampled a birch made out of rattan. Lasts much longer than the real thing. Even on an impudent rump such as yours.'

I showed her the birch, tied in a red bow. She was a little frightened now, but trying not to show it. I prefer the birch because canes are harder to control, however experienced you are. It's quite easy to miss and give someone an extremely painful swipe just where they don't need it... in the middle of their thigh, for instance. No erotic benefit and a sting like sulphuric acid. An exaggeration perhaps but it's a sensation you won't forget in a hurry. As it was, the birch caught her right on the sweet spot. With a few more whacks, just to keep her yelping for more, I picked her up and took her to my bed. It was high time she played with *me*, selfish little baggage.

We spent the next few hours making each other come, rubbing our faces in each other's bodies, snuffling up our mingled earth and sea scents. Needless to say this sweet ecstasy wasn't enough for her. She needed coke and cigarettes more than anything else.

As the bedroom filled with smoke time and time

again I decided that what she needed was a proper caning. I hate smoke!

'Time for you to bend over properly,' I told her. I didn't have to fake the aggression or the cold hatred. She had been boring me with coke babble and a little nicotine breath in your face goes a very long way.

'Come on. Stand up, bend over and grasp your ankles. You need six stripes across your backside, young lady.'

Her eyes glazed over as she stepped into the world I was creating. She staggered to her feet, wobbled a little, wiped her nose yet again, snorted down some coke-drenched snot, glared defiantly and then bent over. I got up and picked out my thickest rattan.

'Grasp your ankles and hold the position.'

She managed it somehow. Now it was impossible to hold back. Her back was arched, her peach was ready and I could resist no longer.

I tried spacing out the strokes, for maximum pain, but the sound of her cries was just too exciting. All too soon I had given her five beauties. She was panting but I still hadn't broken her.

I drew the cane back as far as possible and landed it with maximum force. She jumped up squealing, hopping around the room holding her bottom. She calmed down enough to kiss the cane and then we feasted on each other.

I will always remember that day, long after the stink of cigarettes evaporated. The frenzied love. The talk. The laughter. But the instant she ran out of Marlborough she vanished for good.

Maybe she found a rich Englishman. Maybe she annoyed the wrong person. She could have drunk herself to death or got into heroin.

I think of her often, my Russian ruby. But it's a relief she's gone. I'm old enough to know she would have been a disaster if she had hung around. With age comes wisdom. Or perhaps the fires of madness flicker a little softer.

I was a teenage Satanist. Now I'm twice as old as the little girl who courted darkness. Whenever possible, I seek the light. My skin's still white, my hair is black, but in summer I wear light colours. I still like smacking bottoms of course, all the shades of red my hand can conjure. From the prettiest pink to the deepest vermilion. Suicide now looks like a cop out and as for Sylvia Plath? Thank God for Prozac…

Come Here

Katharine Tyler Brooks

SHE had not turned the lights on when it began to grow dark, choosing instead to huddle in the shadows, curled up in the corner of the sofa, her knees drawn up to her chin. There in the reflected light of the freshly set sun, she waited for him. Her heart seemed to beat twice as fast as usual. Even the sound of the cat padding softly behind her to find its dinner in the kitchen jolted her heightened nerves.

The sound of tires crunching on the gravel driveway made her jump and pull herself more tightly inward. Time was gone. He was home now. There was no escape.

He would pack his things and leave her, just for now, of course, for this was his house. He would leave for a few days while she made other arrangements, moved in with a girl friend or waited for the family to fetch her. It didn't matter. He would be gone from her forever, and that would be like death. It was death.

The key turned in the lock. He kept his house key separate from the others so his key never made a sound except the snap of the lock opening. He stood silhouetted in the doorway, the porch light glowing around his edges.

'I see you, you know,' he said calmly. 'You can't hide.'

She blinked when he flicked on the light. She did not move. She felt him looking down at her from across the room. She could not raise her eyes to meet his. He came all the way into the room and stood above her.

'Look at me,' he said with a calm more frightening than anger.

Hesitantly she lifted her head. His face showed no emotion.

'Come here.'

She knew she could not move of her own will, but his words moved her body for her. With no sense of how she came to be there, she stood before him, looking into his blue-grey eyes, shivering as if the floor were made of ice.

'I told you never to lie to me. I told you it was the one unforgivable thing you could do.'

'Yes.'

'Speak up.'

'Yes.'

'Then why?'

She tried to look away, but his hand gently brought her eyes back to his.

'I was so... jealous. Her voice on the message was so sexy. I thought she... I know there have been others, maybe still are. I erased the message. Then I told you there had been none.'

For a long, terrifying moment he only looked at her, his hand still gently cupping her chin.

'It's about trust, Karen. If we don't have that, all we are to one another means nothing.' He dropped his hand from her chin, squinted, and turned his head away. Suddenly afraid he was about to leave, she reached out and grabbed the sleeve of his wool suit.

'I trust, Alan, please. I trust you. I do. I – it's me. I'm so insecure, so unsure. Sometimes… I'm so sorry.' She could feel and hear the tears in her own throat, but none would come to her eyes. He softly removed her hand from his sleeve.

'You nearly cost me my best client. I'd have lost hundreds of thousands of dollars. And if she hadn't called the office today, I would never have known why.'

'But it's all right now,' she said. She searched his face for her answer.

'Yes. At the office, it's all right. We even had a good laugh over how the answering machine must have eaten her message…'

'But,' she thought. There will be a 'but.'

'There's no harm done, Alan, and I am so very sorry. I promise I'll never do any such thing again.'

His look grew colder, his eyes narrowing slightly. She couldn't help backing up a step.

'How can you say that? There's no harm done at the office, but what about us? The breach of trust, I don't know if I can get past that. A relationship like ours can't exist in a climate of mistrust.'

She felt her soul crumble. It seemed her body itself was falling apart, imploding slowly, cell by cell.

'I had a moment, one weak, childish moment when I doubted myself, but not you, my love, never you.'

'I wish I could be sure of that, Karen, but you've just proved to me otherwise.'

There was a long silence in which neither could take their eyes from the other. Finally, she could take no more.

'Shall I go, then? Do you hate me now?'

Words and arms seemed to reach her simultaneously.

'No, of course not,' he said as he embraced her, caressing her hair as he held her to his chest. 'I could never hate you.'

For a long, long moment, they stood embracing. When he finally released her, his face was calm, resolved. He took her gently by the hand.

'Come here,' he said.

She knew where he led her. She had been there many times before, but never for punishment, only for the games they played that heightened their sex life. Her heart lurched at the thought of what he might do, yet she didn't dare to hesitate. Long ago, she had agreed to be punished as he saw fit. Though she had never thought the time would come, she knew that whatever he had in mind for her was far better than being left.

The room was not the 'dungeon' some might call it. It was neither dark nor austere, merely an extra bedroom fitted with the necessary tools and fixtures for their particular sexual sport. The four-poster bed was somewhat smaller than the bed they slept in at night so that her body was easier to reach from all angles and her arms and legs would not be overstretched. Padded benches and chairs of all sorts were scattered about the room and numerous rings and other bondage tools stood about or were mounted to walls.

Alan went directly to the implement cupboard and threw it open. He withdrew a black satin blindfold. She gasped to see it. Being unable to see had always been her worst fear. Blindfolds had been on her 'red' list, the things she did not consent to. Apparently, that list was not in play this evening.

She shivered as she felt him tie it behind her head.

She felt him check to be sure she couldn't see around the edges. Then he took her hand once again.

'Come here.'

He led her several steps, then stopped. She felt his hands slip under her skirt and pull down her panties. He hesitated at her ankles, and she knew he expected her to step out of them, which she did. In the next moment she felt herself upended, her skirt lifted.

She had expected a spanking. She'd been spanked this way often for minor offences, but usually in the living room or bedroom, not the 'extra' room. Knowing that the location could only mean much more to come, she resolved not to make too much of a fuss over just a spanking.

But the moment Alan's hand struck her bottom, her resolve vanished. Alan's spankings always hurt, but this one hurt as if he were using the paddle even though she knew he was only using his hand. He stung her bottom hard and fast, with no respite to catch her breath as he did in play. By the fifth blow, she was in tears and by the tenth nearly hysterical.

He spanked on and on. Unable to restrain herself, she began to wiggle and kick. He spanked her all the harder until her cries became one long scream.

Finally, he stood her up. She felt him wipe her face with a tissue. Then invisible hands unbuttoned and removed her blouse, her bra, pulled her skirt off over her head. Naked now except for her high heels and stockings, she waited for his next move, trembling both from the spanking she had just received and what more was to come.

'Wait here,' he said.

From his footfalls, she knew he had gone to the

implement closet. The clink of the buckles told her that he was taking out the restraints, though she could not tell what other items he might be taking from the cabinet as well.

'Come here,' he said, as he took her hand and led her through her personal darkness to the bed. She felt the edge of the mattress against her thighs and waited for his command.

'Climb on.'

This wasn't easy since she couldn't see, but she managed to feel her way to the right position and waited once again for his order.

'On your belly – for now.'

She lay with her face on the pillow.

'Spread eagle.'

She stretched her arms out to the sides and spread her legs as far as they would go. She felt his hand push up on her right hip from below, telling her to rise up for her cushion to be placed. When that had been done, she felt him attach the cuffs to each wrist and ankle and secure them to the posts.

There she lay for what seemed like an age, anticipating what he might do next. So far, he had done nothing that they had not done before, but she had never been punished while lying in this pose. The thought of what he might do now that this was not play left her trembling with anxiety, wondering if it would hurt so much more that she couldn't bear it. Would he stop if it became too much? Something deep inside her subconscious, felt rather than thought, knew he'd never give her more pain than she could withstand.

She felt his fingers caressing his handiwork from her

stint over his lap. It didn't hurt much anymore, just felt warm, glowing. No real damage had yet been done.

'OW!'

She cried out as the first crack of some implement she had never felt before struck her ass. What the hell was that?

Before she could breath, it struck her again, directly across the center of both cheeks. If she hadn't been tied, she'd have bucked right off the bed. She felt one of her acrylic nails snap off from the force with which she clutched the pillow beneath her.

'Oh, Alan, please! I trust you. I won't do it again.'

The blows didn't stop.

Alan spoke with labored breath.

'I know you won't do it again, Karen.'

Three stinging swats fell in quick succession as he continued.

'The question is do you really trust me?'

The strap continued to descend, despite tears, screams, and any pleading she was able to manage between breaths. Burn fell upon burn, searing new layers of flesh each time it hit. Still, she dared not cry out the words that would make it stop.

He had moved the dreadful tool down her body so that it now connected with the tenderest area of her bottom, the place where it met her thighs. From time to time, it wrapped and struck her pussy with a sting that resulted in a blood-curdling scream. This seemed to be very satisfying to Alan, because after he had done it a few times, he did it several times in a row, obviously on purpose. Her screams shook the walls, or she imagined that they did.

When her last shattering scream ceased, she realized

she had stopped screaming. The pain continued, but she felt it on a different level, as if it had submerged into a farther corner of her mind. She felt her body relax, her flesh move in waves with the blows. She felt very, very quiet and lay in a state of profound submission even after she realized he had stopped.

Momentarily she felt his hand moving over her bottom, spreading something soothing. She realized it must be the aloe vera gel she kept on hand for burns. The cooling effect was immediate.

'Good girl,' he said quietly. 'That's my good girl.'

He kissed her shoulders and the back of her neck then began to release her from her bonds, finally removing her blindfold. He carried her to their bed and laid her on it, helping her to get under the covers. He turned to go.

'Alan!' she called after him.

'I thought I'd give you some time to recover.'

'I'm fine, Alan, better than I can remember being for a long time.'

'Still, I think…'

She held out her arms to him.

'Come here.'

How Not to Manage Debt

Jean Roberta

'WE'VE had a problem with theft,' Charlotte told me. She was showing me around the old confectionary store that was being refurbished as the Kinky Teachers Club. Needless to say, we weren't planning to replace the old sign with one of our own. So far, we were an informal group of two dozen primary and secondary school teachers who had to meet in secret for mutual protection. None of us wanted to lose our jobs.

'Theft?' I asked. I realized that I probably sounded naïve, but I could hardly believe it. 'Who would steal from our group?'

'Former members,' she answered grimly. 'Naming no names. A certain married couple, Master and slave, conveniently moved away last summer and then we discovered two-hundred dollars missing from the bank account. He was our treasurer.'

I knew the couple she meant and I felt slightly nauseous. 'That's disgusting. I can't imagine why anyone would trade their good names for such a small amount.'

Charlotte, who rarely smiled at anyone, gave me a long, approving look. She was a straight-backed woman in her forties who identified as a switch, but she carried herself like an authority figure. Her dark eyes were clear and penetrating, but her lips were full and soft in a face characterized by a strong nose, cheekbones and an olive complexion. Her mane of long black hair was shot through with silver, and she usually wore it pulled back in a simple tail that swayed when she walked.

I had often been told I was cute and wholesome-looking, with good taste in clothes. I kept my reddish-brown hair short, not having the patience for a dramatic coiffure. I was vain about my girlish figure and the willpower that enabled me to keep it under control in my late thirties. Compared to Charlotte, however, I felt like a small vanilla wafer.

'This is where we're going to put the sling and the horse.' She switched on a dim lightbulb that hung from the ceiling of a back room that looked as if it had been used for storage. It was empty except for several large boxes.

'Will there be enough room?' I couldn't bring myself to ask how elaborate the scenes in this room were expected to be. How many lucky victims would be beaten or fucked in here at one time, and by how many tops? Would a symphony of gasps and screams echo off the walls, or was I just a gullible novice with too much imagination?

Charlotte grinned at me. 'It'll be cozy,' she said, watching my face.

I almost hoped the room was going to be left in its current state of slightly ominous shabbiness, as though the ghosts of the family that lived over the store in the 1940s still lingered. I imagined a teenage daughter of the store-owner backed against a wall by the delivery boy who had finally worked up the courage to kiss her, to stroke her hair and then her breasts. And when she almost fainted in his arms instead of pushing him away, he would raise her skirt and work his fingers into her hot, secret, virgin cunt. And when no irate parent or bolt of lightning came down on their heads, they would feverishly pull off enough of their clothing to fuck like dogs in heat.

'The guys are coming on Tuesday afternoon to refinish the floor. Someone needs to let them in.' Charlotte was looking at me. I had been too lost in my fantasy to catch her drift, but I knew she wasn't making idle conversation.

Like one of my brighter students, I guessed that I was being given an assignment: Charlotte was going to give me a key to the place so that I could let the workmen in. She knew I was still on compassionate leave after my father's death, so I had free time during the day.

'Will you do it?'

'Sure,' I answered. I felt as thrilled as though she had asked me to walk through a door, literally, into a place of honour and respect. 'No problem.'

She pulled a large, rusty key out of her purse and dangled it at my eye-level. I held out my hand to receive it, and she looked at me until I realized that I looked like a naughty child waiting to get the strap across my palm, back in the day when such discipline was not only legal but customary. I blushed, and she grinned.

'Guard it well, Emily,' she told me, dropping the key into my palm.

I guessed that she wanted to see whether I could lock and unlock the front door. Keys and locks, as I knew from experience, could be as quirky as people.

We walked to the front door and out to the sidewalk. I pulled the door closed behind us, inserted the key, turned it until I heard a click, then tried the handle to determine that the door was locked.

'Mm,' muttered Charlotte, almost inaudibly. She seemed satisfied that she had chosen the right person as gatekeeper.

She gently touched my shoulder as I slid into her expensive car, which still smelled like new leather. Of course, Charlotte and her husband Keith (who was also her Master) had two incomes between them, but she seemed like the kind of woman who would have found a way to get the things she wanted, even without help. Faint shivers ran through my body from the place where she had touched me. Something about the way she drove gave me the impression that she would have preferred to have both her competent hands on me than on the steering wheel.

'I'll see you later, dear,' she told me as we sat in front of my apartment building. 'Let me know how it goes with the workmen.' The word 'dear' sent a jolt all through me. She had never called me any such thing before, and it sounded much sexier from her mouth than from my grandmother's. Charlotte meant so much more than she was saying. I knew (or hoped!) that she wanted to own me in some way, but she also wanted to make sure I would make her proud.

'Oh yes, Charlotte,' I told her, hoping I didn't sound like a high school girl on a first date. She smiled slyly as I climbed out of her car to return to the solitude of my apartment, a rat's-nest full of papers and books.

Bisexual, I thought as I mindlessly straightened the mess, as though for inspection. *I am bisexual.* The word hardly seemed big enough to cover all my desires, although I knew it would have shocked my parents down to their bones. That thought made me flinch.

I remembered that my father could never lecture me again, and my mother was unlikely to confront me about anything I did, since she had always tried to keep the peace between her husband and her children, and that didn't leave much room for her to develop firm opinions of her own. My brother and sister had moved away years before.

I had loved and resented my father. I was grieving for him, but his death left me feeling like a free adult.

When I awoke the next morning, the empty clubhouse for the kinky teachers was calling to me. I have always had relationships with particular places, and I wanted to feel the atmosphere of the old store when no one else was there to distract me.

I drove to the rundown neighbourhood where the building stood on a corner lot. For a moment, the front-door lock refused to yield, but I had come prepared with a bottle of light machine oil, and I anointed my key with it. 'Come on,' I muttered, almost like a lover, as I jiggled the handle and twisted my little tool in the rusty lock. The door opened.

I walked from room to room, noticing the faded roses on the old wallpaper on one wall, and the cracked oak baseboards. I knew that oak was the wood of choice for local antique collectors. Someone had probably lived in this building at one time. Someone had taken care of it.

I almost felt stroked by invisible fingers as I pulled open the top drawer of a splintered wooden bureau. The drawer contained police-style handcuffs, a ball gag, a blindfold, a hood and a few items I didn't recognize. The second drawer contained a flogger, a cane, a riding crop and other implements that I didn't dare touch, knowing that they belonged to someone else.

An unmarked envelope, tucked into a corner of the drawer, looked more inviting. There was nothing in it to indicate its owner or its purpose, but it was stuffed with ten chocolate-brown Canadian hundred-dollar bills. I felt as if I were being tempted by the Devil.

I had gone into debt for my father's funeral. I knew that Mum couldn't afford it, and no one else in the family had offered to help. No one seemed to care whether I could meet my own living expenses.

I had a week to wait for my next paycheque, and then I could replace the money from the envelope. *I would never steal*, I thought, *but everyone I know borrows money from somewhere, especially when coping with emergencies. By the time this building is fit for play parties*, I thought, *the money will be back in its place*.

I left the envelope where I found it and left the building with the cash tucked into my wallet. I told myself that the only reason I didn't leave a signed IOU note in the envelope was because I hadn't brought any paper with me.

During the next few days, I spent money on sensible things: overdue bills, groceries, a credit card payment. Then I bought myself a set of black lingerie: bra, panties and garter belt, plus a pair of sheer stockings. I told myself that I needed such things for when I would play (blush) semi-publicly with other members of the club. I didn't want them to be repelled by my old, cheap underwear which was never meant to be seen.

Anxiety kept me company, day after day, no matter how hard I tried to convince myself that I was not a thief. I looked forward to Tuesday when I could welcome the workmen into the new clubhouse as though I owned it, and supervise their work.

The two guys cheerfully introduced themselves as Frank and Joe. 'Who bought this place?' asked Frank. 'Church group, is it?'

I couldn't think of a glib answer, so I muttered 'um.'

'I heard there's a bunch of perverts in town who bought an old store so they can have orgies in there and do sick stuff like whipping each other where no one can hear them,' said Joe. 'You're not involved with that, are you, honey?' He seemed to be studying my breasts.

I broke out in a sweat. I was outnumbered by two physical labourers who could easily overpower me. 'It's a teachers' club,' I said too stiffly.

Frank plugged in a machine without pausing for breath. 'I thought the teachers' club was over on Slate Street,' he remarked. I didn't respond.

The men refinished the floor with impressive speed and covered it with a protective layer of varathane. Joe straightened up and looked at me expectantly. 'You're paying us, right?'

I felt faint. 'I thought you'd send us an invoice,' I tried to say firmly.

'Nah,' said Joe. 'The lady who hired us said she'd leave money in an envelope where you'd find it so you could pay us in cash. No one gave us an address where we could send a bill.'

Just when I thought things couldn't get worse, Frank stood up, looked around the walls and the ceiling, then snickered. 'You've got some tight security in here,' he told me, staring up at a corner. I followed his gaze and saw the tiny surveillance camera. For once, I had no idea what to say.

Somehow I managed to convince Frank and Joe that they would be paid for their work within a month. To show them how trustworthy I was, I wrote my name and telephone number on the back of a business card that Joe handed to me. I didn't want to give him the name of the school where I taught. When Frank asked for my home address, I didn't see how I could refuse. I wrote it next to my phone number. I might as well have added, 'Available any time.'

I returned home, feeling sick with dread. I had thought of my apartment as my cozy nest and the old store as a haven from the ignorant, vanilla world, but now I couldn't feel safe anywhere. For a few moments, I seriously considered leaving town, at least for awhile.

Charlotte phoned me while I was trying to eat a salad. I had no appetite for anything heavier. The sound of her voice brought me a kind of horrible relief.

'Emily,' she started with no preliminary pleasantries, 'I think you have something to tell us.' The plural pronoun increased the turmoil in my stomach, if possible.

'Yes.' I couldn't find any other words for her.

'Several of us have discussed the situation and we've decided to have an emergency meeting at the clubhouse in half an hour. You'll be there to let us in.' It wasn't a question.

'Yes,' I repeated. 'I'll be there.'

'Emily…' She paused. 'I am very, very disappointed.' She sounded hurt, and I could feel an answering lump in my throat. 'I can't imagine how you could justify what you've done.'

'I can't, Charlotte.' I couldn't afford to say too much because I was desperately holding back tears.

'Well, we'll discuss it further. I'll see you.' With a click, she dismissed me.

I was wearing my new lingerie under my clothes to give myself confidence. I thought of changing into something less provoking (sackcloth and ashes) but realized that I couldn't afford to be late for my fateful appointment.

Driving to the clubhouse, I clutched the steering wheel with white knuckles. Luckily, I arrived first and let myself in. The space no longer felt welcoming.

There was a sharp knock on the door. When I opened it, my heart sank. There stood the entire executive of our club: Charlotte and Keith (who was the President), Bruce (another Master), Eva (a Mistress) and Thomas (a switch). No one was smiling. There were no submissives in sight, even though Eva had two of her own. This was the discipline committee.

I couldn't look anyone in the eyes. I was tempted to grovel on the floor, but was afraid of being hauled to my feet and slapped for overacting.

'Emily,' growled Keith, a tall, bearded, muscular man in workmanlike black jeans and a faded grey T-shirt. I was reminded that this was an impromptu, private meeting. 'You know why we're here.'

Keith's air of forcefulness had made me nervous even before this evening. Not knowing where to rest my eyes, I glanced at the surrounding witnesses. Charlotte looked so sad that my gaze quickly moved on to Bruce, who was standing next to her. He was a short, stout grey-haired man who could spank women into quivering jelly. He looked angrier than I had ever seen him.

Plump, blonde Eva usually laughed easily, but now she looked serious. I thought I saw sympathy in her blue eyes, and that gave me hope. I couldn't help noticing the cleavage that showed between the buttons of her tight red blouse, and wondered how many of her teenage students had been distracted by her full breasts. Realizing that I probably looked impudent too, I dropped my eyes.

Thin young Thomas was at the edge of the group, sullenly rubbing his boots together. As an underling, he pushed his luck, and while topping someone (usually another man), he pushed his victim's boundaries. His presence felt iron-cold to me.

Keith was holding out one hand. Of course, he wanted me to return the money.

I tried to speak, and burst into tears instead. No one moved. Wetting my face, my sweater and everything in my purse, I dug through the jumble and found three-hundred dollars which I held out to Keith. Charlotte took the money while I continued my search. I came up with six dollars in coins, which I poured into her waiting palm.

The silence was unbearable. 'That's all I have left,' I blubbered, wiping my eyes. 'But I'm not a thief. You have to believe me. I meant to replace it all as soon as possible.'

'We believe you,' said Keith, to my surprise. 'But why didn't you say a word to any of us? Or leave a note explaining your intentions?'

'I... I didn't think you'd find out.' I felt cold sweat at my armpits and hot shame in my heart.

'You have two choices,' said Keith. 'Return the key, leave here tonight, and we'll report your theft to the police. And you'll be banned from the club.' When I didn't respond to his offer, a look of evil joy flashed across his face. 'Or take your punishment from us and stay in. On probation.'

I was terrified, grateful and scalded with guilt, all at once. 'I'll take punishment from you, Sir. Sirs. And Madams.' My legs felt so shaky that it was a relief for me to kneel.

'No safe word, girl,' Keith warned me.

'I understand, sir.'

He reached down to seize my sweater and roughly pull it over my head. Cool air hit my skin as everyone looked at my new lacy black bra.

'Dressed to impress,' remarked Bruce sarcastically.

'Take all your clothes off,' Keith ordered. 'You need to be searched first to make sure you're not hiding anything.'

I stood up awkwardly to unzip my skirt and step out of it. As I stood in my underthings, I saw an unmistakable bulge at Thomas's crotch, and Charlotte looked amused. All of them reminded me of hungry cats watching a frightened mouse.

A feeling of surrender spread through me like hot oil, and settled heavily in my cunt. I had never believed that fear and arousal could coexist in me, but the growing wetness in my panties was a sign of my undeniable excitement. I was afraid that everyone in the room could smell my womanly musk.

I unhooked my garters, rolled my stockings off, and continued taking off every stitch until I was completely naked. I knew without looking that my sensitive pink nipples were puckered to hardness.

'Go face the wall,' ordered Keith, 'and hold onto the hooks. Don't move until I tell you to.'

A pair of rusty metal clothes hooks stuck out of the back wall; apparently this room had once been someone's bedroom. I had to stretch my arms to reach up and grab both hooks. I knew that this pose would be hard to maintain for long, but I didn't dare complain.

Calloused, knowing hands ran down my sides and familiarly over my buttocks, making me squirm. I jerked when a hard male belly and a harder cock pressed into my back as a different pair of hands squeezed my breasts and fed each of them into a pair of tight nipple clips. I gasped. 'These will hold your attention, girl,' snickered Bruce.

A man's long fingers spread my lower lips apart and deliberately stroked my wetness as if to test my arousal. Then three hard fingers thrust into me, stretching the skin at my opening until it stung. Large fingertips (Keith's?) probed my cervix and rubbed my inner walls. I felt completely explored, known and taken.

'Come for me, little thief,' purred Keith, surprising me with his generosity. 'We'll see if you like what comes next.' This threat sent me into a crashing, uncontrollable orgasm. I danced on Keith's fingers while he continued to fuck me with them.

The witnesses began to clap in time. *Clap! Clap! Clap!* I couldn't help thinking of the punishment to come, as they surely intended. I came twice more, feeling almost hysterical. My possessor withdrew, but the search wasn't over. A slippery, greased finger invaded my ass, burrowing deeply into me as my muscles tried to expel the invader.

'Relax if you don't want it to hurt, Emily,' said Charlotte. I felt humiliated to the core, but I concentrated on obeying her. Before long, she had two fingers in me. She seemed to be reaching up into my guts to discover my most secret desires.

Without warning, someone pulled both clips off my nipples and I came again from the shock.

Just when I thought the ache in my arms would force me to lower them without permission, Keith said 'You may lower your arms and turn around.'

Having to look at the whole committee was almost worse than hanging from hooks. For better or worse, the next phase of my punishment was a lecture.

'Emily,' Keith started, much gentler than I expected, 'you've disappointed all of us, but we're sure you've disappointed yourself more. You know you could go to jail for what you've done. To satisfy your conscience, I'm going to make it hard for you to sit down for awhile. Remember that we're doing this for your own good. If the consequences didn't suit the crime, you'd despise yourself for a long time. We're going to help you end it.'

'Thank you, sir.' Tears were flowing from my eyes again.

'Bend over and hold your ankles.'

I did as I was told. Through my hair, I could see the women in front of me, while the men gathered behind my upraised ass.

Whack! The pain was like fire in my flesh but I remained silent. *Whack! Whack!* I guessed that Keith was using his belt. By the time he finished, I was sobbing and suspected that he had raised blisters.

'Stand up.'

I straightened up slowly, aching in all my muscles. 'Oh, sir, it hurts.'

'It's supposed to,' he told me calmly. 'Bruce and Thomas, hold her.'

The two men leered at me as they held me upright by the shoulders. This time, Keith used a cane on me. I screamed and bucked at the first stroke. The second released hot liquid from a cut across my ass, and I knew he had broken the skin. I learned later that he gave me seven strokes, one for each of the unrepaid hundred-dollar bills. By the time he finished, I was almost fainting.

Cool ointment was stroked onto my burning skin, but the gentlest touch renewed my agony. 'You'll heal, bad girl,' promised Eva, 'and then you can earn the money back. You'll practice with us.'

Through the roaring in my ears, I heard Charlotte explain that I had been traded to Frank and Joe to pay for their work; it was all arranged. I was going to be their kinky whore for an evening, and they had promised to keep it a secret.

I guessed that I would have to please the executive committee with my mouth and my cunt, but the worst of my punishment was over. My shame would not be made public, and I knew I would be a better person from then on. Like something else I had heard about in church, being forgiven felt more precious than rubies.

Hard Times

Sarah Veitch

CONSTANCE shivered as the warden led her towards the governor's office. 'Don't dawdle, or it'll be all the worse for your backside,' he said with a malicious grin. Constance knew that he hated her more than most because she was of good breeding, had education and sophistication on her side.

The warden knocked and the Governor called an abrupt 'Come in.'

Constance pulled herself up to her full five foot three and tried to look imperious. How she wished she wasn't wearing this hateful prison dress, an ankle-length slate grey. Once she'd have turned heads with her fashionable leather shoes and calfskin booties, but now her feet were unpedicured and bare.

'What brings you here?' the Governor asked when she reached his desk.

'To prison?' Her father had died leaving gambling debts so she'd stolen repeatedly to continue living as a lady. A five year term in this London gaol was the end result.

'No – what crimes have you committed since?'

'None,' Constance said haughtily.

'Failure to work,' said the warden. 'She's been here a

week and already ignored her laundering duties twice.'

The older man looked her up and down. 'Prisoners have to work to pay for their keep. What have you to say for yourself?'

'I was tired, sir. I needed respite.' Couldn't he see that her soft, manicured hands couldn't cope with clouds of steam and rough lye soap?

'Your soft hide shan't earn respite from the birch,' the Governor replied. He wrote something in the ledger before him then looked intently at his employee. 'Give her twenty lashes now and the same next Friday, Warden Neath.'

As Constance watched, the men exchanged satisfied smiles, then the warden gave her a little push towards the doorway. Soon she found herself stumbling through a maze of hallways until they reached a large square room with a stout woman lounging by the door.

'Fetch the prison doctor, Matron – I'm about to make this girl sing for her supper,' Warden Neath called out.

'Not before time if you ask me,' the woman replied, staring at Constance, 'Thrash out some of her la de da ways.' She glanced at her colleague. 'D'you want to get her stripped and spread out nice and wide, love? Me and the surgeon will be back in five.'

'My pleasure,' Warden Neath said. He watched Matron leave then turned to Constance. 'Right, poppet, let's get you bared for the birch.'

Constance hesitated, but he was stronger and heavier than she and could call for back up. *Best to act proud and indifferent*, she told herself, *refuse to let him see that you're afraid.*

'As you wish,' she said haughtily, and pulled off the

faded garment. Using all of her willpower, she kept her hands at her sides though she was desperate to cover some of her nakedness.

'Your titties will bounce nice and high when you're flinching under the lash,' the warden murmured, his eyes feasting on her flesh.

What were titties? As usual, he used language that Constance hadn't previously heard. She'd been educated at her father's knee throughout the 1870s, but doubted if this man – who, at around thirty, was more than ten years her senior – had been educated at all.

'Present your bottom for the birch,' he continued, pointing at the heavy metal frame which dominated the room. The nineteen year old stared confusedly at the contraption. 'Not used to it, obviously,' he continued, almost as if talking to himself, 'Well, all that's about to change.'

She shivered as he grasped her right wrist and led her to the frame. 'Your feet go here.' Constance followed his instructions, sliding her bare feet into shoes which were fixed to the stone floor. He immediately tightened them so that they held her motionless. 'Now you bend over here.' He pushed her over the thickest metal bar as he spoke. 'Then we hold your wilful little wrists together and attach them to this.' He clipped her wrists together with iron fetters then attached the fetters to a bar in front of her that was about one foot from the ground. Now the top half of her body was bent forward and held firmly, her bare buttocks obscenely presented for the birch.

The teenage thief quivered with anticipation and shame as the female warden and a well-dressed man – obviously the prison doctor – entered the punishment room.

'What's she here for?' the doctor asked casually.

'Twenty on her arse today and the same next Friday,' Warden Neath replied.

Constance shivered anew as she felt a surprisingly rough hand stroking and palpating her helpless fundament, examining the swell of her rear cheeks and the silken slope of her thighs. 'Such a small, round bottom will mark up mighty prettily,' the doctor said when he finally finished exploring her proffered hemispheres, 'And she'll be kicking like a mule when you thrash her again in a week.'

'She'll not kick with her legs pinioned,' the warden answered with some satisfaction. 'Nor lash out with her arms when they're so nicely fettered to the frame.'

'Aye, she's not going anywhere,' Matron cut in, beginning to walk towards a large container in the corner that held two hateful-looking birches and other punitive implements. 'Let's put these twigs to work and make her backside dance a jig.'

'Don't be too hasty my love,' Warden Neath said, and Constance could hear the expectancy in his voice. 'I've got me something different from my brother in The Americas. They use it in the prisons there and it's guaranteed to make grown men beg.'

'This beauty with the leather blade?' the woman asked, pulling a punisher with a two-foot-long handle from the jar.

'Ah hah. It's called a paddle. Slap it against your thigh and see how it stings.'

The woman did then winced and examined the implement further before handing it to the warden. 'My, that will certainly show an uppity bitch who's boss.'

Constance stared at the hellish punisher and wondered how it would feel on her nubile extremities. As the others disappeared behind her, she realised she was about to find out.

'Stroke one,' the jailer said, and Constance felt the air currents shift as he drew back the hateful paddle. Seconds later, an explosion of heat radiated through her raised bottom and she cried out and writhed in her bonds. She was still trying to get her breath back when she heard the words 'stroke two' and her backside radiated wildly again.

'Stroke three.' She tensed up her bottom the little she could then squirmed as the paddle bit into her flesh. 'Stroke four.' This time her wriggling was more protracted, each movement grinding her naked tummy into the metal bar.

'She's pink already. She'll be glowing like a hot coal by twenty,' the doctor murmured.

'A *sizzling* coal,' Warden Neath clarified in a gloating voice.

The pain was bearable but was clearly going to intensify. Maybe she should give the impression that it was too much for her and they'd halt or lessen the punishment? Constance prepared to give the performance of her life.

'Stroke five.' She screamed when they laid it on and pulled impotently at the wristlets.

'Stroke six.' Her impassioned wails echoed around the punishment room.

'I see we have an actress in our midst,' the doctor murmured.

'Not for much longer. I've been building her up

gradually but now I'll really give her something to cry about,' the warden said.

Constance held her breath then let it out in a genuine wail as the paddle exploded across her upturned bottom. God, that had hurt far more than the previous strokes.

'Stroke eight.' Another thick streak of fire raced across her tethered hemispheres.

Crying out, she tried – and failed – to pull her feet from the special shoes which held her so cruelly in situ. She'd longed for shoes from the moment she arrived her last week, but now she yearned to be walking barefoot down the corridors, to the laundry – *anywhere*.

'I'll work,' she cried out desperately.

'Aye, but you'll work with a tenderised arse,' Warden Neath countered in his coarse East End accent. She sensed that he was admiring her hot bare bottom. 'Reckon my brother was right about using this to liven up the ladies,' he continued, obviously addressing the room in general. 'This one's already jerking harder than most old lags do under the birch.'

'Aye, she's wriggling like a new-caught eel,' murmured Matron.

'And gasping like a landed fish,' the doctor said.

She wouldn't wriggle or gasp again, Constance told herself as she tried to regain her composure, *she just wouldn't*. She'd bear the rest with dignity, even aplomb. But, even as she thought the thought, her backside twitched of its own volition and she heard the Matron laugh.

'Who'd have thought a peach could turn such a pretty crimson?' Warden Neath murmured.

'Or beg so nicely,' Matron said.

'Stroke nine coming up. Oh sweetheart, you're not going to be acting when you taste this one.' He wasn't kidding. Constance cried out loudly as the paddle slapped mercilessly at her proffered expanse. Her belly was now pushed so hard against the bar that it felt like she was being dissected. How had someone like herself, a lady of the parish, been reduced to this?

'Stroke ten.' She shook her bottom from side to side the little she could, but it was obvious that it wasn't going anywhere. Her piteous groans echoed around the room and she gasped again and again that she'd do as she was told.

She'd do as she was told all right, or her arse would be permanently bent over the whipping frame. Warden Neath stared contemptuously at the naked prisoner, wailing like a banshee when she was only halfway through her punishment. Two of his sisters had ended up in gaols across town for stealing bread when they were close to starving, whereas this bitch could have lived simply off the proceeds of the family house. Instead, she'd stolen to fund a more lavish lifestyle, and now refused to earn her keep in this women's gaol.

'Dr Grant, if you can just check on the prisoner's condition?' he said with false solicitation.

'My pleasure,' the other man replied with a throaty laugh. Neath watched as he stepped forward, admired the teenager's bare body for long moments then ran his palms over her tethered flanks. She shivered violently at his touch then moaned low in her throat as his palpating increased the pain in her tender parts. 'She's a healthy mare who can take much more punishment,' he confirmed eventually, slapping at both cheeks and making the prisoner howl.

'I can't!' Constance gasped loudly, 'Oh please, sir – really I can't!'

'I shall continue my ministrations to make sure,' the prison doctor replied, and Neath watched as he slipped a finger into the miscreant's pleasure-hole and thrust it in and out, making the naked young woman groan anew. 'All responses are normal,' he clarified, licking his finger, 'And she's ready to taste the paddle for another ten.'

'Please, I can't bear it,' Constance gasped.

'Really? In that case, a more thorough investigation is called for,' the man replied, slowly inserting his middle finger into her served-up anus. As he thrust it in and out, Constance squirmed at the odd sensations and the blush which suffused her body testified to her increasing shame.

'Has a man ever availed himself of this part of you?'

'No, sir. How could he?' the prisoner whimpered.

'A girl who truly can't take any more is exhausted, can't tighten her sphincter,' the doctor said, adding a second digit to the first.

Constance cried out. 'No more – you're cutting me in half!'

'As I thought, all fine and dandy,' the man concluded slowly withdrawing his fingers from her widened orifice. 'Warden, you can continue thrashing these lazy little cheeks.'

'If you insist, doctor,' the warden said, exchanging a smile with the Matron who, as usual, was pushing her own right hand against her uniform, palpating the area between her thighs.

He picked up the punisher again, knowing that this

was his favourite part of the session, the second half. By now, the girl bent over the frame knew exactly what a thrashing felt like, was desperate for respite. He only had to scrape the birch against the ground – as he was doing with the paddle now – for the troublemaker to pucker up her disarmed bare bottom. He only had to move his arm and make the air currents change for her to push herself desperately against the metal bar.

'Stroke eleven,' he announced but made her wait, in an agony of anticipation, before he applied the dreaded punishment. This time the paddle went low, marking both the underswell of her cheeks and her thighs.

'Stroke twelve,' he continued. 'I think I'll lay this one further up.'

'I can't bear it,' Constance protested.

'Of course you can – doctor says you're a healthy filly with an arse that's made for punishment.'

'But…' She broke off as he toasted her burning backside again.

He waited, tapping the paddle against his outer leg, until she calmed down: experience had shown him that it was better to wait until a girl was concentrating on her sore buttocks, dreading the next judicious application to her recalcitrant flesh.

'Thou shalt not steal,' he murmured.

'I won't ever again, sir. I swear!' She sounded as if she meant it.

'Your bottom will remind you not to.' Raising the paddle, he warmed her orbs for the thirteenth time.

'Thirteen, unlucky for some,' Matron murmured then doubled over briefly, right hand working overtime. My, but that woman loved to see an uppity girl squirm.

Sometimes she came twice in a session, and he was willing to bet that she played with herself again afterwards at the memory. He was looking forward to taking care of himself in private when he'd finished correcting Constance – and, judging by the bulge in the other man's trousers, he wasn't the only one.

'Number fourteen coming up, though I'm running out of space. Maybe we should feed you up with bread so that you've got a bigger backside for future thrashings?'

'I'm never coming back here,' the wrongdoer promised in a quaking voice.

'Sorry, but your arse isn't getting off that lightly. You're coming back here next week at the Governor's orders,' Neath replied. He loved the fact that the Governor often meted out such double punishments as they ensured that the prisoner worked hard for the next few months.

'Time to remind that naughty bottom who's in charge here.' He administered the fourteenth stroke and watched Constance's bare backside flinch and pucker, only to briefly smooth out then flinch some more. By this stage, every iota of her being must be concentrated on her helpless hindquarters, her every move given over to trying to shake off some of the pain. He knew that she'd give anything to cup her flaming buttocks, had already decided to leave her wrist fetters in place for the rest of the day.

'Fifteen.' He could see that Matron was touching herself again and his own manhood ached painfully at the unfolding tableau. This time he lashed the paddle into the centre of her raised rump, watching it flatten briefly as the thick leather slapped hard. As ever, there was a second when the offender went beyond words then she began an impassioned wail.

'I'll do anything,' she said.

Warden Neath glanced at the others and they both nodded encouragingly at him. Release was imminent! He walked, stiff leggedly, to the front of the frame. Getting down on his knees was equally difficult with such a large erection to contend with, but he eventually positioned himself so that he was lower than her face.

Unbuttoning his trousers, he placed the tip of his manhood close to her lips. 'Your bad behaviour makes him very sad – but you could kiss him better.'

'Kiss who? What?' The girl opened her eyes and stared blurrily down at him.

'My friend here.' He pushed his hardness between her lips. 'Just give him a little lick and he'll be fine.'

He exhaled hard as he felt the girl's soft mouth enveloping the very tip of his cock then sighed with frustration as the contact ended. 'You have to keep going – unless you'd rather have the paddle instead?'

The warning seemed to work and she mouthed inexpertly at his root, kept doing so. He came quickly, and suspected from the sighs and groans across the room that the other two had done the same.

'Good girl,' he said, getting shakily to his feet, 'As a reward, I may not lay on the last five so hard.'

'But I thought...' Constance muttered, staring at him dazedly.

'A wayward girl shouldn't think – only feel,' Neath countered, reminding himself that her soft lips had enjoyed the finest rouges whilst his sisters had often lacked basic clothing and housing. She'd had five minutes respite from the paddle. What more did she want?

'I could lick the doctor,' Constance said.

Neath looked at him quizzically but he shook his head. 'I'm here to oversee – and anyway I'd rather watch her wriggle under the flogger.'

In reality, the warden knew that the man was already spent. He glanced at the Matron, knowing that she'd love to position her female parts under Constance's warm, wet tongue, but knowing also that it would never occur to the teenager that this was an option. And, as Matron was much too proud to suggest it, she'd have to miss out. Matron fared much better with the older girls who knew that tonguing her cunt or her titties brought them favours or at least an early respite from the birch.

It was odd starting again after such an enjoyable interlude. He stared at the bottom before him, served up for punishment, and wondered if he had the energy to do it justice. Wardens usually made a first punishment especially memorable so that a mischief maker saw the error of her ways.

The Matron seemed to read his thoughts. 'Shall I do the honours, warden? Thrash that naughty little vixen for tempting you?'

Neath nodded gratefully, realising that he liked the idea of a spectator sport. He watched as the older woman fingered the leather punisher for long, loving moments before lining it up with the prisoner's trembling backside.

'This will teach you not to tease your elders and betters,' she murmured before swinging the paddle into the girl's upturned flesh for stroke sixteen.

The renewed sensation after the hiatus must have hurt more as Constance's cries echoed around the room and she tugged impotently at her bonds and again promised anything.

'Anything?' Matron asked hopefully.

'Lick the doctor,' Constance gasped as she had before.

Matron scowled. 'Four to go,' she mumbled after counting and recounting on her fingers.

'Fear not, dear lady, it's my duty to keep a tally,' the doctor said.

'Doctor, please, I can't take any more,' Constance whimpered.

'Miscreants don't have an option,' Matron said.

Neath knew that the older woman loved to take her frustrations out on the girls. He made sure that she went easy on the genuine hardship cases, those who had stolen in order to ward off starvation or to feed their children. But work-shy ladies like this one deserved a hot, sore arse.

'Seventeen.' The woman laid the blow over the offender's central swell, doubtless reawakening earlier paddle strokes.

Constance howled.

'Eighteen.'

Another wail.

'Nineteen.' By now the same flesh had been roasted again and again by the leather blade, the paddle also marking the top of the girl's thigh backs.

'Ask me nicely for the last one,' Matron said, running the leather across the gentlewoman's helpless flesh.

It seemed to take Constance a while to find her voice then she said 'Please use the paddle on me again, Matron.'

'Say *please warm my naughty little cheeks, Matron*,' the older woman elaborated.

Sobbing with humiliation, Constance mumbled 'Please warm my naughty little cheeks.'

The Matron obliged and she cried out into the punishment chamber then sobbed some more.

'Admirable as the view is,' Warden Neath said softly, after a full five minutes of staring at the naked prisoner, 'It's time I took her back to her cell.'

He did just that, tethered the young mischief maker to her bed and hurried back to the punishment room.

'She's tied down on that soft belly and is feeling very sorry for herself. But not as sorry as when her cellmate returns from the laundry, I'll bet!'

'Serves her right, letting the other girls do her share of the work,' Matron cut in. She was looking rather flushed and Neath privately wagered she'd been rocking against the stool that she sat on, a covert way of pleasuring herself again.

Neath winked and turned to the other man. 'Well, doc, did we treat the prisoner fair?'

Neath's mate grinned. 'I doubt if the real doc would have let you use that paddle.'

'Fortunate for us that he's in his cups as usual and you were able to stand in.'

'Stand in? Hell, I was doubled over by the end. You know there's nothing gives me more pleasure that seeing a pretty young reprobate being taken to task.'

'So, same time next Friday?' the warden asked.

Neath's mate and the Matron both nodded eagerly.

'No chance of the Governor popping in halfway through?' the woman asked nervously.

Neath shook his head. 'I found out from a friend the other day that he prefers boys, is always over at the

House of Correction. He likes to see these young lads take the birch.'

'So we can use what we like?' Matron confirmed.

'Uh huh, we can do our own thing as there's no one to supervise us. Personally, I'm glad of the change, was tired of using the birch.'

'All these twig ends,' Matron said with a shudder, 'I was forever sweeping up.'

'So, how do we warm Constance's arse on Friday?' Neath's mate asked.

'With a cat-o'-nine-tails,' Neath said happily, 'My brother sent it to me, says that just one stroke leaves nine hot weals on a bad girl's bottom. I'm looking forward to laying it on hard.'

She must think positive, Constance told herself as she lay tethered on her softly rounded stomach. For once she was glad that her cell's tiny window didn't have a shutter, for the cold breeze had cooled her punished cheeks. The paddle had been terrible but at least she'd be familiar with it on Friday, would know what to expect. And surely the doctor would intervene if Neath or Matron went too far?

She wondered when Neath would return to untie her from the bed. Four hours must have elapsed as she could hear the other women returning from their morning shift at the laundry. Molly, her cellmate, was a hard woman but might show some sympathy, bring her a crust of bread.

She turned her head sideways as her cell door swung open.

'Molly. I'm so glad to see you!'

'As am I to see you,' Molly answered, sitting down

on the side of the narrow bed. 'We had to do all your work as usual.'

'I'll make it up to you tomorrow,' Constance said. She trembled as she realised that the other girl was staring at her exposed bare bottom and flexing her muscular right arm.

'You'll make it up to me now – and later with that pretty pink tongue of yours,' Molly said, beginning to spank with a surprisingly firm palm.

For Writers Only

The stories which you have just read were winners in Palmprint's first four annual CP short story competitions. After judging each comp, I wrote a report which appeared in the publisher's mini-spankzine *Submission*. I've reproduced them here in the hope that they'll help new erotica writers, especially those who enter writing competitions.

Sarah Veitch

2003 Competition

At first they arrived singly, large manila envelopes spaced apart by days or even weeks – but as the closing date for the competition neared, there were three or four in every post. Some came from the furthest reaches of Canada and America, whilst others made the relatively short journey from parts of England, Ireland or Wales. Surprisingly, Palmprint didn't receive an entry from Scotland, the home of the tawse.

The presentation was excellent. Only one writer used such a faint typewriter ribbon that his manuscript was almost illegible. Everyone else typed or wrote very clearly, making their entries a joy to read.

Most people had also taken on board the erotic theme and had lots of sex in their stories, but one scribe had written a literary short story and merely added a half dozen lines of CP towards the end!

Several of the stories were good enough for, say, an internet spanking site or even a spanking journal where the editor may only read three or four stories a week. But competitions are somewhat different. After all, the judge will be sent dozens of such competent stories – you need to produce something different to stand out from the crowd.

By the second day of judging, I found that the same themes were cropping up multiple times. There were lots where two female friends suddenly decided to try lesbian sex. They either included CP in this or were caught by one of the girl's boyfriends, who proceeded to punish them. Another much-used theme was where two couples who were friends decided to spice up their marriages by having sex together. Again, this involved CP. A third set of stories involved CP sex whilst on holiday in an exotic location whilst a fourth subset explored being caned by the boss. Stories set in cyberspace were also popular, but unfortunately this distances the reader from the action. Reading about someone who is reading text on a screen doesn't make for a very arousing narrative. That said, a truly accomplished writer can make even a hackneyed theme sound exciting – but none of these stories screamed 'choose me.'

Several writers were so keen to make their stories a hundred percent consensual that the erotic aspect was lost. As such, the man would say 'please spank me', his wife would spank him and she'd then suggest that she should have six spanks to even things up.

A variation on this theme occurred in stories where one partner recognised the other's subconscious love of spanking, at which they spoke about it as such length that there was hardly any space left for the spanking itself! *Show don't tell* as all good writing tutors say.

Other stories involved more unusual settings but lacked continuity. As such, a man would pull a woman over his knee, remove her knickers and give her a bare bottom spanking. But a couple of paragraphs later he'd somehow manage to pull her knickers down again! Similarly, a character would be gagged in one paragraph and we'd be told that she could only make muffled noises – but a little later in the story she'd shout out several clear sentences. Had the gag been removed then? Well, no, because a few paragraphs later we'd be told that her partner was now removing the gag. Such breaks in continuity occurred so often that I started to mark them up as I read each story so that I could easily edit them for sense if they won a prize. But some editors and competition judges will simply reject a story like this in favour of one which the writer has proofread properly.

I'm not making these points in order to patronise new writers. Been there, got the T-shirt. I can remember one editor who scrawled the following over the first page of my carefully crafted short story: 'sounds autobiographical and I didn't care enough to read on.' And a girl I attended creative writing classes with was told by a famous writer that 'most people have a manuscript or two under the bed. Yours should stay there.' She was devastated and didn't write again for several years. So, rest assured, I'm pointing out common themes etc so that writers can bring a fresh perspective to, say, Palmprint's next competition or to other comps.

All of the stories had some merit. Several reached the shortlist and it was with sadness that I eventually put them aside. They were wonderfully descriptive but lacked erotic content or had first class dialogue but came to an abrupt or unsatisfactory end. Virtually everyone had at least a few good phrases or a section of highly erotic action or some other talent. Some writers admitted they were sending their first ever story – and their entries were refreshing in their level of reader-identification and general honesty. One such new writer was planning an entire series based in cyberspace. She showed promise but is more likely to prosper if she finds a more immediate setting for future erotic prose. I'd like to thank her, and everyone else who entered, for their hard work. Palmprint also deserves a round of applause (pause for the sound of one hand clapping) for creating one of the few competitions around which doesn't have an entry fee.

So, on to the winners! One of the big problems facing any erotica short story writer is how to get to the CP action quickly yet still make the journey believable. Michael Redbrick of London, who I've awarded the £100 first prize to, gets around this problem brilliantly by making his entry a speech by the proctor of a women's reformatory – a speech that's devoted to discipline. This allows him to supply the reader with an erotic charge from the second paragraph without losing credibility. He expertly builds the reader's arousal by describing the many ways that his nubile charges can be corrected and maintains this arousal by literally piling on the erotic agony.

The £50 second prize goes to Tulsa Brown for *Goddess*, the most technically accomplished story I had the pleasure to read. It's a perfect crime story with an erotic-domination setting. *Goddess* is also as well-written as contemporary literary fiction yet it has what most literary fiction lacks – a plot and, moreover, a twist in the tail. This clever story deserves two or three readings to fully appreciate its nuances. I'd have awarded it first prize if the CP had been more frequent and overt, more arousing. But that distinction definitely goes to *L'Ancien Régime*, a story to curl up with on a cold winter's night.

The £25 third prize is awarded to Suzee Moon and Stan Strap for their collaborative effort *Way Out West*. Suzee and Stan succeeded in choosing an unusual setting – a bar in Tombstone – with a no-nonsense sheriff who enjoys administering a spanking. So when the new curvy hostess steps out of line... After lots of erotic talking down there's a public spanking followed by a more private punishment.

2004 Competition

The postie definitely looked in need of a chiropractor by the time he finished delivering the mail for this year's competition. Envelopes arrived from America, Australia, Canada, England and Wales – though, as with last year, there were no entries from Scotland. There again, the Scots are probably too busy paying for their Parliament to afford a stamp...

Naughty girlfriends and errant wives featured in many of the stories and disobedient secretaries were another favourite. Many of these were well-written and deserve to end up in CP magazines but they weren't quite special enough to win a comp.

Roleplay was another common theme, with variants of strip poker which included punishment featuring especially strongly. But one of the more unusual stories involved a roleplay centring around noir films.

Other unusual themes included a story told from the viewpoint of a soft toy and one narrated by a criminal-turned-nun. It was fun to read such original texts, even if the stories weren't convincing enough to win.

There weren't many competition rules – but it was surprising how often people broke them. Several entrants were over the 4000 word count with a few even attaching little notes saying 'I know that I'm over the word count but…' Others ignored the rule that all characters had to be adults and wrote distasteful scenes in which mothers and fathers punished their teenage daughters.

Another rule which several writers ignored stated only one entry per person. When people sent in more, we read the first story we fished out of the envelope and discarded the others. But a harsher taskmaster would have disqualified that entrant from the competition without reading a word. Palmprint's competition is free, but most competitions charge a five pound entry fee so getting disqualified is a somewhat costly mistake.

Quite a few entrants seemed to have taken a vanilla story which was already in the word processor and simply tacked on a CP ending. One eleven page story didn't have any discipline until page nine!

Stories which centred around the writer's most-desired sexual act were often very well-written. Unfortunately the preferred act was often fellatio rather than any form of corporal punishment.

One of the stories was beautifully written and erotic

but I couldn't quite figure out the plot line after two careful readings. Another started strongly and was erotic throughout but the author had adopted the 'you do this' format and after several pages the constant 'you then' approach began to grate. But both writers showed talent and may well succeed at a later date.

So on to the winners. I awarded first prize to Stan Strap for *Cat Fight at the Lucky Seven* because it was highly erotic. It also engaged me from the first paragraph and – a bonus but not essential – made me smile several times.

The author sets the scene in the first paragraph, provides humour in paragraphs two, three and four, and by paragraph five he's straight into the action. And he stays with that increasingly-orgasmic action until the very last line.

Second prize went to Kit for her story *Disobedience à la carte*. Kit grabs the reader's attention with her opening sentence of 'When will you learn to be obedient?' Thereafter she offers a beautifully-written literary story about a CP love affair. The characters are realistic, the writing atmospheric, the observation sharp.

Third prize was awarded to J.D. Jensen for *Disobedience, Passion and the Unjust Whip*. This is erotic historical fiction which builds up a keen sense of anticipation. Will the lovely Aquistana feel the lash of leather on her naked flesh?

I'd like to thank everyone for entering the competition and giving me and my clitoris hours of reading pleasure.

2005 Competition

This year – for the first time – we had entries from France, Greece and Scotland, and, as with previous years, stories from America, Australia, Canada, England, Ireland and Wales, most of which were beautifully presented and competently written. Many deserve to find homes in spanking magazines.

On the downside, several entrants deserve a smack for breaking the rules, some doing so in multiple ways. A few people sent in stories that were thousands of words over the maximum limit. One man even sent in a book-length manuscript. Others sent in two stories despite the fact that the rules stipulated one. In these instances, we entered one story for the competition and discarded the second – but most competition organisers would have filed the entire contents of the envelope in the waste paper bin.

A few entrants were so obsessed with retaining their rights that they'd typed out odd statements like 'withholding all the copyright for all the purposes.' But the rules stated that we had the right to print the winning entries in Submission and consider them for an anthology at a later date.

Two people sent in the exact same story as last year – either they'd forgotten that they'd done so or they hoped that standards had fallen. Another sent in an entirely vanilla story, yet a quick look on the internet would have given her the definition of CP. At the other extreme, some of the punishment scenes amounted to torture – and incest also reared its ugly head.

Thankfully there were lots of enjoyable erotic stories

to balance the extremism, with every permutation imaginable from chastising threesomes to punitive governesses and from play-dungeons to errant maids.

But there could only be three winners, and I awarded first prize to Aimee Nichols for *The Mercy of Strange Men*. The title is intriguing and the rhythmic opening of 'Lydia is ready. Lydia has been ready for some time' draws the reader in. It's followed by a very believable description of the difficulties of being in bondage for a prolonged session.

The story continues in this focused way, is literally wall to wall CP from first paragraph till last – in contrast, many of the stories I read used up six or seven pages before introducing any punitive atmosphere or action. *The Mercy of Strange Men* is also superior in that it looks at punishment from both the Master and slave viewpoints. The reader is therefore drawn into Lydia's 'sub space' and into her Master's mindset and desires.

The second prize-winner is Alicia Wag for *Lessons*, a compelling story about a sexually-submissive college student who finds the courage to go to her dominant male tutor and hint at what she wants. The submissive Cindy presents as a believable character rather than as simply a cipher for the humiliating events.

Third prize goes to James Baron from England for *Beloved Birch*, one of several male sub stories we received. Most were of angry wives (or their best friends) punishing errant husbands and were competently written, but James' story was unusual in looking at a judicious birching administered to a confirmed masochist. Again, it's a hundred percent focused CP.

My grateful thanks to everyone who entered the

competition for giving me lots of hot reading on equally hot summer nights. I'm already glistening in anticipation of next year's erotic offerings.

2006 Competition

First, the good news – the winners of this year's Palmprint Erotic CP Short Story Competition demonstrated their love of the genre and their commitment to good writing. Bruce Anderson, who came first with his male-dominant *Think Pink*, brought a light touch to his story which didn't detract from the arousing punishment scenes. He focuses on Suzie's correction from the very first sentence to the not-so-bitter end. Second place went to Mark Ramsden with *Rubious* who didn't let the lesbian element overtake the vital discipline. He also writes in an entrancingly authoritative voice. The third prize was taken by Katharine Tyler Brooks for *Come Here*, an atmospheric vignette about a dominant male and submissive female which is rounded off very nicely at the end.

Sadly, there were fewer promising stories than in previous years. Most of this year's entries were of lesbian punishment – or rather, lesbian cunnilingus with a few paragraphs of spanking or paddling thrown in. Sometimes the chastisement didn't appear until the end of the story and it was clear that the entrant would have preferred to pen non-erotic prose. The lack of hetero stories might also have been due to political correctness, with entrants confusing erotic spanking with domestic violence. But I've said over and over again (I've even begun to bore myself!) that the two acts are worlds apart, so if they'd bothered to do a little research...

One woman hadn't even bothered to research what CP means, as she sent in a hundred percent vanilla story. We get at least one such entry every year. We also received dozens which had several small words missing per page or where a character's name would start being spelt differently halfway through. We've all made a few such errors as the eye sees what it expects to, but when there are ten to fifteen on each page it's clear that not even the most rudimentary proofreading has taken place.

Many years ago, I submitted an article to a magazine and they rejected it with a helpful compliment slip. It contained several pre-printed phrases with adjacent tick boxes, with themes ranging from *You Can Write But Need To Target Your Market Better* to the damning but honest *Never In A Million Years – Do Something Else*. In my case they ticked the box *Try Again In Six Months*, which, in retrospect, was fair. Sometimes, when reading the poorest stories, I wanted to tick the *Do Something Else* box – after all, these entrants might be brilliant at painting, acting, double-glazing, anything which doesn't involve words.

Yet some of the entrants could write, had simply chosen a hackneyed subject. So here's my suggestion list to help entrants craft their stories for other erotic CP competitions:

Concentrate on the CP rather than lesbian oral sex / literary flights of fancy / lesbian dating agencies / vanilla sex / lesbian mutual masturbation / ramblingly long descriptions of the weather / lesbians online. This isn't an anti-lesbian rant – but the competition is for erotic *corporal punishment* prose, not girl on girl action with a token three smacks thrown in. The very few male dominant stories stood out amidst a sea of sex-but-little-spanking femme2femme.

Put your story aside for a fortnight after writing the penultimate draft then return to it with a critical eye. Have you written in sentences? Given questions a question mark? Remained consistent with the characters names and descriptions? Kept to within the word count? Only submitted one story as stipulated? Used a large and dark font that won't strain the poor judge's eyes? (Sarah said, reaching for the tea bags again.)

My thanks to past and present prize-winners for fulfilling these criteria and more, and for restoring my faith that today's writers can produce well-written and stimulating prose.

About the Authors

Bruce Anderson (Scotland) is the pseudonym of a self-employed businessman who currently lives in the north of Scotland. He wrote regularly throughout the 1980s for American CP magazines but stopped when they introduced new writing guidelines that were too politically correct for his taste. Bruce remains an avid reader of spanking novels though admits he often secretly feels that he could do better if time permitted. He prefers to write punishment scenes which aren't infused with romance. Bruce is happily married but jokes that, upon retirement, he'll treat himself to a Thai bride. His current wife – who he refers to as the first Mrs Anderson – thinks otherwise.

James Baron (England) has spent much of his career in show business, and is the author of several novels and contributes to various magazines both in the UK and overseas. While working in Rome, he wrote a screenplay *C'e Stato un Incidente* which is in pre-production.

Katharine Tyler Brooks (USA) is a writer of BDSM erotica living in southern California. Her works have appeared in *Just Us Girls* and *Men Under Control* (CF Publications). Her story 'Marie' has been published in *Working Hard* (Mondadori). She also writes science fiction, Arthurian romance, and magazine and web articles about BDSM and BDSM toys.

Tulsa Brown (Canada) is a recently escaped novelist from another genre, who's having a sinfully good time in erotica with her fiction appearing in many anthologies and magazines. Her family believes she's writing something scholarly. Shh.

Sarah Dean (England) has a career in media and her first novel *Bound for the Top* (Chimera) was published in 2006. She is widely travelled and a keen equestrian, skier and tennis player.

James Hamilton (France) provided the cover drawing for this book and is an Irish artist, currently living in France. He studied Fine Art in England in the mid-1980s and that is when he developed a growing fascination for the beauty of the female form, both in and out of the life-study room. Returning to Ireland and the financially difficult profession of being a painter, he began to use his skills gleaned from the life-model for privately commissioned illustration work of a sensual nature. This work continues to the present day, as well as illustration work done for publishers in Britain and the United States. James is still available for private commissions and can be contacted through Palmprint Publications.

J.D. Jensen (England) was born on a farm in Kenya and orphaned when his parents were killed in the Mau-Mau uprisings. Sent to live with his alcoholic and sometimes violent uncle in South Africa until his death in a light aircraft crash, JD was bundled off to become a boarder at a home run by a Catholic brotherhood. After making a meagre living at various precarious jobs, JD eventually came to Britain at the age of twenty on a Portuguese freighter, working his passage as a deckhand.

Now, some thirty years later, JD is Operations Director of a fleet of cargo ships. Four times married, but single again, JD boasts that he 'knows a pretty woman and a comfortable berth' in almost every major port in the World. He writes in his spare time, always with a glass of cheap brandy at his side, and his black African bull's pizzle-whip – a gift from an Arab trader – on his desk. He says: 'I've seldom ever met a girl who… in the heat of the moment… ever declines a friendly spanking, always provided that it is followed by furious lovemaking and with a liberal dose of affectionately wicked laughter.'

JD is the author of *A Cruel Passing of Innocence* and several novellas about the adventures of a French countess, convicted of fraud and sent to Devil's Island.

Pearl Jones (USA) writes erotic fiction of several stripes, some of which may possibly be based, at least in part, on personal experience – or not. (Incubi? Sea lions? Shrink-wrapped vegetables?) All names have been changed to protect the guilty; innocents need not apply.

At present, Pearl may be chained to a keyboard and typing madly away. Or she could be chained elsewhere. The sad truth is, she's probably feeding a refrigerator on feet sometimes referred to as a cat, but writers are known for their rich fantasy lives, so let's go with artisan-crafted silver links and a handsome alpha to crack the whip… metaphorically or otherwise.

Kit (England) is a medievalist who also writes fiction, songs, plays guitar and practises Tarot. Publications include 'Perfect' in *Erotic Tales*, 'Changing Roles, Changing Rules' in *Best S/M Erotica 2*, 'Power Cut' on www.desdmona.com and 'MMF' in *Binary: The Best of Both Worlds – Bisexual Erotica*.

Ruby Kola (USA) is the pseudonym of a writer based in Wisconsin.

Suzee Moon (Wales) is a large, curvy forty-something Welsh woman who enjoys reading, writing and looking at images of moderate spanking. She particularly enjoys romantic, workplace and domestic settings. She has a background in education and management but has recently given up full-time employment to work on several writing projects.

Aimee Nichols (Australia) never quite got the hang of polite conversation. She is a student and freelance writer, which means she spends a lot of time sitting in front of a computer with her head in her hands. Her work has appeared internationally in anthologies, magazines and online. Further information can be cobbled together from www.intergalactic-hussy.net

Mark Ramsden (England) wrote an acclaimed black comedy trilogy for Serpent's Tail featuring a short over-opinionated American Dominatrix and her English lover:
    'Delightful' The Guardian
    'Agreeably distasteful' Sunday Times
    'Dryly witty' Skin Two
    'An excellent novel. Very, very funny' Headpress
    'Uh?' the general public
He is the inventor of Fetish Morris Dancing.

Michael Redbrick (England) is a four-times published author, who also works as a freelance journalist and advertising copywriter. His pen has earned him a living all his life. His fascination with corporal punishment was roused in the seventies when he discovered Janus and Roué, and he has always tried to get away from stories where the girl commits a misdemeanour, is called to account, and thrashed.

Married with two children, his wife indulges his interest but is determinedly vanilla and doesn't read his punishment stories. An sm book he submitted to a US publisher in 1990 needed revisions and still languishes in his filing cabinet.

Jean Roberta (Canada) torments the young by teaching first-year English courses at a Canadian prairie university. She sings in a gay/lesbian/bi/trans choir, Prairie Pride Chorus, which has produced *Watershed Stories*, its first recording of original music. Her erotic stories have appeared in over fifty print anthologies including *Best New Erotica 6*, *Best Lesbian Erotica* and *Wicked Words*. Her BDSM lesbian novel *Prairie Gothic* was published by Amatory Ink. Visit www.jeanroberta.com for details.

Stan Strap (Wales) is a rather fierce Welsh-man of Irish descent. He spent his whole working life in education and training but has now taken early retirement to study drawing. He is a keen practitioner of the art of spanking, especially in a domestic setting. He has always enjoyed writing all sorts of fiction but his spanking stories are particularly inspired by, and dedicated to, Suzee Moon.

Sarah Veitch (England) is the author of six CP novels and three CP short story collections. She writes much of Palmprint's spankzine *Submission* and maintains a website at www.sarahveitch.com

Alicia Wag (USA) has been published in *Natural Health*, *Mousie*, and the *Beloit Fiction Journal*. She recently started writing erotica, and loves every minute of it. She has stories in *Best Women's Erotica* (Cleis) and the online journal *Clean Sheets*.

Also available from Palmprint Publications

Subculture by Sarah Veitch
ISBN 0953795306 A-format paperback, 252 pages, £9.95

Lisa's work takes her to Malta – where she finds that her new employer, Dr Landers, is a strict disciplinarian. He soundly canes and tawses the girls who work at his deluxe Health Clinic and lets his senior receptionist spank the younger staff. The doctor is intriguing and Lisa is hugely drawn to him. If only he didn't resolve every dispute by pulling down her pants…

Will she reluctantly submit to the rod and reach new vistas of shame and ecstasy? Or will the obstacles she faces send her fleeing into a more conventional lover's arms?

Corrective Measures by Sarah Veitch
ISBN 0953795314 A-format paperback, 308 pages, £9.95

* A shy Russian bride has to taste the whip on her wedding night
* The model in a spanking video betrays her producer so badly that she has to submit to the cane for real
* A young woman breaks the law in a futuristic setting and endures having her bottom bared before the state caning machine…

These 21 stories demonstrate a wide range of punishment implements and judicious settings. Here many young women – and two unfortunate young men – pay at length for their intransigence. The collection also includes the mini novella Re-educating Ruth in which a young female infidel reluctantly agrees to spend several months at a merciless House Of Correction for adulterous women in Amsterdam.

Below the Belt by Sarah Veitch
ISBN 0953795322 A-format paperback, 303 pages, £9.95

Kerri is duped into moving to Alpineglow, a remote town with a unique brand of justice. She arrives to find it's owned by Jeff Rendell, a man she once seriously wronged.

Jeff and his overseers strictly discipline Kerri and the other disobedient dissidents. They're also set exquisitely-demanding sexual tasks.

Permanently nursing a sore bottom, she searches for ways to exploit the system. But her cunning tactics lead to increased humiliation for nothing is exactly as it seems…

Further Training by Sarah Veitch
ISBN 0953795330 A-format paperback, 192 pages, £6.95

Charlotte winced in sympathy as the Colonel pulled down the girl's shorts. Like her twin, she clearly favoured commando-style. Her naked quarters looked incredibly vulnerable on the whipping stool. She was swiftly bound to the device and her superior picked up his cane.

Charlotte is such a disobedient slave that she's transferred to island two of a vast correction centre. There, she's strictly re-educated at the shame-based school and military academy until she pleads for clemency.

In this sequel to The Training Grounds, Charlotte comes up with a scheme to thwart her superiors. The only drawback is that she'll be assigned to the sadistic Karo if the plan backfires…

Reformed Characters by Sarah Veitch
ISBN 0953795349 A-format paperback, 275 pages, £9.95

* Two boarding school girls enrage a punitive janitor and suffer the consequences
* A young female serf incurs her Master's wrath
* A budding novelist contacts a dominant female writer with unexpected results
* A holiday rep earns a severe tanning
* Three pretty but dim girls join Carly's Angels, an unusually strict detective agency

Numerous naughty females and several disobedient young men are forced to reform in these seventeen tales of transformation, Sarah Veitch's third adult punishment collection.

Sarah Veitch's Submission

Submission is Sarah's spankzine launched in 2002. Subscription to this mini-mag offers readers letters, news, reviews and interviews plus Palmprint's annual prize short story competition. Submission is only available direct from Palmprint by mail order or via www.palmprint.co.uk

Palmprint books can be ordered from all good bookshops and are available from amazon.co.uk and amazon.com. To receive our catalogue, send a stamped, self-addressed envelope to:

>Palmprint Publications
>PO Box 392
>Weston-super-Mare
>BS23 3ZS
>United Kingdom